He was in rampage mode

It was time to stop playing by the enemy's rules, and to start doing things his way. Mack Bolan had never been the kind of man to sit back and allow the savages to assault him.

The plan was simple; one the Executioner had used countless times before.

Lean on the enemy. Lean on the enemy's friends. Lean on the enemy's enemies. Apply as much pressure as possible until his target popped into view.

Then drop the hammer.

D0696146

MACK BOLAN ®
The Executioner

6:40

The Executioner®
Don Pendleton's

EDGE OF HELL

Gat Van Zoy

Josephine

Baumgartner

BAX

uc CDB

E. Lake

208 31

363 Lorne

A GOLD EAGLE BOOK FROM
WORLDWIDE®

TORONTO • NEW YORK • LONDON
AMSTERDAM • PARIS • SYDNEY • HAMBURG
STOCKHOLM • ATHENS • TOKYO • MILAN
MADRID • WARSAW • BUDAPEST • AUCKLAND

First edition December 2005
ISBN 0-373-64325-X

Special thanks and acknowledgment to
Doug Wojtowicz for his contribution to this work.

EDGE OF HELL

The god of war hates those who hesitate.
> —Euripides: *Heraclidae* ca. 425 B.C.

Even as I stand at the edge of hell, I will not hesitate to take action against the enemy.
> —Mack Bolan

THE
MACK BOLAN
LEGEND

Nothing less than a war could have fashioned the destiny of the man called Mack Bolan. Bolan earned the Executioner title in the jungle hell of Vietnam.

But this soldier also wore another name—Sergeant Mercy. He was so tagged because of the compassion he showed to wounded comrades-in-arms and Vietnamese civilians.

Mack Bolan's second tour of duty ended prematurely when he was given emergency leave to return home and bury his family, victims of the Mob. Then he declared a one-man war against the Mafia.

He confronted the Families head-on from coast to coast, and soon a hope of victory began to appear. But Bolan had broken society's every rule. That same society started gunning for this elusive warrior—to no avail.

So Bolan was offered amnesty to work within the system against terrorism. This time, as an employee of Uncle Sam, Bolan became Colonel John Phoenix. With a command center at Stony Man Farm in Virginia, he and his new allies—Able Team and Phoenix Force—waged relentless war on a new adversary: the KGB.

But when his one true love, April Rose, died at the hands of the Soviet terror machine, Bolan severed all ties with Establishment authority.

Now, after a lengthy lone-wolf struggle and much soul-searching, the Executioner has agreed to enter an "arm's-length" alliance with his government once more, reserving the right to pursue personal missions in his Everlasting War.

Prologue

She stumbled out of the bed, sheets snarling around her feet. Her hands broke her fall, and she swore she heard something pop in one wrist, but no pain was worming its way up her arm. The high hadn't worn off yet. The floor was cold and bare, good for mopping up ink, coffee and bloodstains.

The sheets finally released her ankles and she slithered free, pulling herself to her knees. The buzz rolling around her bloodstream wasn't done yet, but she was already feeling the panic in her chest, and the twisting of her gut, demanding more release. She had to get dressed quickly and head back. She brushed her hand across her stomach, one fingertip finding the odd itch in her navel, all along the freshly mended flesh of some kind of scar. In her befuddled mind, she wondered what that was. She didn't shoot in there, she shot inside her thighs, where no man would look, let alone put his mouth—at least none of the men who paid her for the company they sought.

She reached for the pile of clothes, yanking aside the man's jacket in her rush to get to her own stuff, but she paused when she felt the weight of the wallet clump across her knee. It was heavy, which was always a good sign, and she tore it open, looking within, as if she expected to find food inside.

There was money, enough pound notes to choke a horse. She crumpled them in one hand and reached for her miniature purse. They would help her out. Trembling fingers let go of the wallet, dumping it flat on the floor, and for a moment, she feared he'd wake up.

She struggled to her feet, slipping her legs through the tiny vinyl shorts she'd bumped and ground so seductively to get the man to come to bed with her. He didn't tell her his name, but she knew the kind of man he was, old money or some governmental import, a stiff conservative type who repressed his sexuality to the point that he was almost ready to explode. Those were the types who gave her most of her business.

She bent over double. Her stomach was sick, as if there were a solid lump of lead inside it. Her balance gave out and she grabbed the doorjamb, barking her forearm. The fresh pain cut through the haze of her dizzied brain and nausea for a few moments. Then she twirled back into the haze.

She couldn't find her baby-T in the dark, and she didn't want to hang around any longer. Something started to smell in the room, and her instincts told her to leave.

She grabbed her jacket and shrugged it over her shoulders, tugging it down and closed to cover her breasts. She hoped that nobody would catch her before she got home.

Home was a swirling morass of half-remembered images. Once she got some fresh air, or at least London air, into her lungs, she figured she'd feel better. Her head was pounding, and she could barely maneuver her feet into her calf-length boots. When she bent to pull the zipper up on one, she tumbled to the floor again.

Bile rose in her throat, and she spit a wad onto the floor. Vile sourness permeated her mouth, but she wasn't sticking around even to wash it clear. She bent and yanked up the zipper on the other boot and staggered back to her feet. Pain raced through her body like a jet of flame, but she managed to make it down three flights of steps without tumbling to her death or falling and breaking a leg.

The front desk was abandoned, and she thanked a God she wasn't sure she believed in. Some bit of vanity made her not want to know what she looked like, at that moment. Nauseous, limping, wishing she was dead, she opened the door and a cool breeze hit her face. She closed the door tightly behind her and leaned back against it, gulping lungs full of air.

It wasn't much, but the sweat soaking her skin had been whisked away, or at least nullified by the misty fog resting at street level. She looked both ways and tried to remember where she was.

Houses were packed tightly together, roads twisting at angles to each other. She could walk for a whole night before finding a path out of this maze. She shook the thought from her mind.

People lived here. All she had to do was pick a street, start walking and keep going. She had to keep an arm out to stay upright.

The road was quiet and empty, and for that she was thankful. If there were any potential customers still out…

I'm not a bloody whore. The thought came to her in a disjointed jumble.

She tugged her jacket tighter around her.

She heard footsteps behind her and turned, seeing a tall man, dressed in a long flowing coat and what looked like a top hat. She knew she had to be seeing things.

He was upon her in an instant, his hand reaching up for her throat, catching and closing around it in a viselike grip. She tried to squeak a cry for help past her constricted windpipe, but she was shoved down a causeway between buildings, her heels skidding as she tried to resist the strength of his pull. Her hands slapped at his forearm, but he wasn't letting go.

That's when she saw the flash of a knife.

Then she remembered why she was sick, why she couldn't focus, and who this man was.

But by then, the Ripper was already beginning his grisly work.

Mack Bolan was nearing the end of the night's grisly work. The iron grip of his hand clenched tight around the sentry's throat, his Hell's Belle Bowie knife plunging deep into the viscera of the mobster, all eleven inches of razor-sharp steel perforating and carving organs with ease. The man gurgled as the Executioner twisted and pulled the knife through his aorta, blood bubbling through half-dead lips before he was lowered, still twitching, to the ground.

There was never anything pretty about the work the Executioner did, but when it came to using a knife, that was some of the ugliest work of all. Even with the opened chest and belly of the guard facing away from him, Bolan could smell the hot, coppery scent of blood mixed with the stench of opened bowels. He concentrated on wiping the blood from his knife to prevent rust and stink sticking to the war blade, ruining its cutting strength and stealth fighting ability.

Sonny Westerbridge had mobbed up hard. The Bolan Effect was going according to plan—a series of skirmishes that raised the heat, forcing the enemy to draw all his resources together to protect himself. It was an old tactic, so tried and true that the Executioner could have plotted the maneuvers in his sleep.

"Hell!" came an angered cry off to his left, an unnecessary reminder to the soldier that while he could run a strategy like clockwork, all it took was one wrong glance at the wrong time to send things awry.

Stealth flew away on the wings of the guard's cry, but Bolan's sound-suppressed Colt spoke anyway. The lack of muzzle-flash from the weapon, and the muffled sounds would at least make the man in black that much harder to spot. A triburst of 9 mm slugs tore open the British gangster's chest and throat in a straight line going up his breastbone. An un-fired pistol clattered from the corpse's unfeeling fingers just before he tumbled facefirst into the ground.

"They're coming in from the west! Move in!" Wester-bridge's voice crackled from the dead sentry's radio.

Bolan was caught between cursing the big London gang-ster and giving him a greater helping of respect. The soldier always respected that his enemies could kill him at any time. He never thought of himself as immortal or bulletproof. And Westerbridge had been prepared for him, springing a trap.

Bolan grabbed the radio off the dead man and stole into the darkness behind a couple of cargo containers as men moved with precision, covering one another as they began to swarm the lot. Crouching, the Executioner disappeared into the shadows, checking the odds against him.

"It's just one man," someone spoke up over the radio, and Bolan spun, diving from his hiding spot. Bullets sparked on the steel of the container he'd crouched against moments be-fore. Leveling the 9 mm submachine gun with one hand, he triggered a burst from hip level, driving the two mobsters back behind their own cover.

Around him, gunners cut loose, their weapons speaking in the dark. He counted muzzle flashes, getting up to fifteen.

"Is that positive?" Westerbridge asked.

"Just one man," came the answer.

Just one man, Bolan thought. Keep thinking that and lose your advantage.

"I don't care, keep up the pressure," the mobster said. "He's done enough damage for a small army."

Bolan decided to punctuate that statement with a special delivery from an attachment under the barrel of the submachine gun. Bolan had chosen the 9 mm Colt for two reasons— one was his familiarity with the line the Colt was descended from—the other was the weapon's forearm was identical to the short-barrel M-16s favored by Special Forces. This made mounting the M-203 grenade launcher easy.

He triggered the first 40 mm shell at a point where a heavy concentration of muzzle-flashes originated. Six ounces of explosive core burst a shell of notched razor wire with terrifying effect. Once the thunderclap faded, screams of agony could be heard from wounded men.

Confusion coursed over the radio's speaker, and the Executioner burst from the shadows, racing to the cover of another cargo container. Gunfire lapped at his heels, sparks rebounding off steel and concrete as he made a final, desperate dive for the protection of the huge trailer.

Two more gangsters swung around the area where Bolan had been moments before, but instead of finding their prey pinned down, they realized they had exposed themselves too soon. The Colt burped again, two salvos of slugs smashed into Westerbridge's men, sending them into the next life.

"Everyone, switch to the alternate channel!" Westerbridge called desperately. The radio suddenly went dead.

Bolan knew Westerbridge was smart and he was scared. Most of the time, the Executioner could count on scared being more powerful than smart, mistakes giving him an easier path to victory. That was in an ideal situation, though.

Gunfire hammered the container he was behind, keeping him from popping out on either side to fire off another grenade. It was obvious that the gangsters didn't really like the idea of being blown to shreds.

The Executioner slung the Colt, braced himself, then sprung for the top of the container. He gripped the edge and hauled himself up, looking for signs of other shooters who took to elevated fields of fire. There were two, at separate corners of the warehouse roof. Swinging the Colt around, he targeted one through his Aimpoint sight. Holding high against bullet drop, he stroked the trigger and planted a burst into the head of one gangster. Considering he was holding for center of mass, he was glad for any kind of hits. He swung toward the other gunner, who jolted at the sight of his partner going down.

Bolan's night-black penetration clothing had made him nothing more than a dark smear against the roof of the container, one more shadow against other shadows. Westerbridge had radios and automatic weapons, communications and coordination, but he lacked night vision for his men.

A wild spray of gunfire rained on the container, but Bolan targeted the muzzle-flash, held slightly lower this time and drilled the other shooter.

The sound suppressor on the Colt made the signature of his kills imperceptible above the sporadic suppression fire clanking off the rolled steel construction beneath his feet. He stuffed a fresh 40 mm shell into the M-203, gave the Colt itself a fresh stick of Parabellum rounds and worked to the middle of the roof.

Westerbridge didn't have night vision, but as the Executioner rose to his feet, staring down from the high ground at the London hardmen who had doubled in number, he did find that Westerbridge had lights.

Suddenly, everything was bathed in the yellowed, tired glow of dozens of lamp units. Two groups of men were caught out in the open, trying to flank what they thought was Bolan's position, but the Executioner himself was instantly bathed in the harsh illumination, a tall, terrifying figure in black, festooned with lethal weaponry and grim resolve.

Bolan triggered the M-203 into the group on his left, then swinging the Colt to his right and holding down the trigger, ignored the blast that hammered into the heart of the squad of shooters. Body parts and weapons flew, chunks of shattered asphalt also raining on the containers around him, rattling like a brief hailstorm.

The Executioner held down the trigger, fanning the stunned and shocked second group, peppering them with a different kind of hailstorm—a barrage of high velocity, copper-jacketed hollowpoint rounds that punched and tore through flesh and bone, swatting bodies off their feet. The gunmen below struggled to regain their footing, scrambling for their lives, trying to avoid the lethal marksmanship on display.

The Colt finally locked empty, and the ragged troop of mobsters gathered themselves. Those who escaped the grenade blast with minor wounds and the effects of the concussion were already turning toward Bolan, weapons brandished, ready to give the man in black some payback now that he was empty.

The Executioner simply let his weapon drop on its sling, hands diving for the Beretta 93-R and Desert Eagle in a practiced double-draw that had carried him through countless such fights. In three steps, he was airborne, dropping off the edge of the cargo container. The handguns hammered out 9 mm and .44 Magnum missiles as the shooters aimed where he'd been only a heartbeat before. It wasn't the most accurate use of his handguns, but Bolan was at close range, and he was working on instinct and a lifetime of practical experience. Whenever the muzzle of one of his handguns intersected the body of a fighting enemy, he pulled the trigger, dropping the gangster in a heap with a high-powered bullet through a vital organ.

The Executioner wasn't standing still. He was charging his

foes, moving among them and between them, so that when they turned to shoot at him, they would also catch themselves in their own cross fire.

The Desert Eagle locked open empty and he let the big hand cannon fall to the ground, snaking his arm around the throat of one gangster. With a shrug, Bolan swung the mobster across the front of his body, a living shield that was instantly greeted by a burst of gunfire.

Bolan jammed the still-loaded Beretta down the front of the dying gunman's waistband, shifted his grip on the would-be killer and clutched the Englishman's right hand, which was holding an Uzi. His trigger finger pressed down his shield's finger, and the Uzi opened up on another gunman who pumped round after round from a heavy revolver into the mortally wounded man. Bolan could feel the spent energy of bullets sieving through his shield's bloody torso into his armor.

The soldier spared the shooter a second burst of 9 mm slugs from the borrowed Uzi, then heaved the dead man aside, using the handle of his Beretta as leverage to spin the corpse into the arms of another gangster charging into the fray. The man dropped his weapon to catch what was left of his partner in crime, then looked in horror down the 9 mm muzzle instants before a single shot sent his brains vomiting out the back of his skull.

Bolan pivoted and dropped to one knee, dumped the almost empty magazine from his Beretta, slapped home a fresh one and continued to look for targets. He flicked the 93-R to burst mode, swatting two more mobsters off their feet with triple-shot salvos of supersonic slugs.

And then it was over.

The silence was deafening.

Bolan reloaded the guns he had on him, then went to retrieve his Desert Eagle from where he'd thrown it down. He checked the battlefield which was the cargo container yard, eyes surveying the carnage. Each body was checked to make sure it was dead and out of the fight. Using the partially spent Beretta, Bolan finished off those who were wounded and suffering from his grenade attacks, giving them a final pill to release them from their pain.

Westerbridge wasn't among them.

Bolan picked up a new radio and listened to the mobster barking orders. What was left of his hardforce was bracing themselves, getting ready to repel the Executioner when he came for them in the warehouse.

The warehouse that an Interpol agent had lost her life trying to locate. Her murder had drawn the Executioner's attention. Inside, Westerbridge was trafficking in everything from heroin to enough small arms to equip a small army. That traffic had cost a fellow warrior her life.

Bolan hadn't known her personally. Neither had Hal Brognola. But Westerbridge was a vermin the Executioner had been intending to visit with a torch of cleansing flame. Other missions had popped up, delaying his actions.

And now, a cop was dead.

Bolan thumbed a 40 mm antiarmor shell into the breech of the M-203, targeted the loading dock doors and fired.

The explosion was sudden and violent. Two mobsters standing near the doors were thrown aside, a third almost cut in two by a quarter ton of steel slamming into his torso.

SONNY WESTERBRIDGE WAS pulling open the crate when the dock doors were hammered off their hinges by an invisible freight train of force. He was startled, but the surprise didn't leave him flat-footed or numb.

Westerbridge hadn't fought his way to the top of his organization only because he was six foot eight and 320 pounds of pure muscle. He was a man who fought for every bit he owned, learning every angle, his brain as formidable as his physical form. He wasn't going to let some asshole in black take everything he had and flush it into the sewers.

Ham-sized hands wrapped around the grips of two Ultimax light machine guns. Built in Singapore, they resembled beefy Thompson submachine guns, just like in the old American gangster movies. Except, instead of holding pistol bullets, their big, fat round drums held one hundred rounds of high-powered 5.56 mm NATO ammunition capable of slicing a person in two.

Westerbridge slung two of the machine guns, then pulled out two more. These were on top of the big Smith & Wesson .44 Magnum revolver he wore in a shoulder holster.

"By God, you fucking son of a bitch, you're not going to take me down without a fight!" he shouted at the phantom fighter.

Gunfire rattled as two more of his shooters opened up on the shattered entrance. They swept the dock with automatic fire, making it inhospitable for any living creature trying to get through. Westerbridge's instincts, however, warned him something was wrong.

The regular access door beside the opening suddenly kicked open, and the bastard in black stepped through, his weapon spitting a red pencil of flame, barely visible in the backlighting from the lot. Westerbridge watched another of his men spasm, pierced in a half-dozen locations.

"Eat shit and die!" Westerbridge snapped, lifting one Ultimax in his beefy hand and spraying an extended burst at the doorway. Sparks flew, chunks of wall and crates exploded in puffs as the mysterious attacker dived out of harm's way.

The massive gangster sidestepped on the platform, held out his other hand and pulled the trigger on the other Ultimax, hosing the area where he thought his assailant was going to be with a stream of 5.56 mm slugs. Instead, he chewed up empty floor.

A round object sailed over the crates as his men took up firing positions. The gang boss bellowed a cry of warning, but the ball bounced and disappeared in a flash of thunder, smoke and chunks of shattered humanity. Westerbridge swung both guns back to where the grenade originated, holding down the trigger and shooting through the crates, splintering wood and denting metal with his firestorm of slugs. Even his thick, powerful arms ached from controlling the weight and recoil of the light machine guns. Sweat soaked through his suit as he cut loose with a throat-ripping roar of fury.

A shadowy form flashed around one aisle and Westerbridge sidestepped, taking cover behind a column of stored military supplies. He checked the load on both Ultimaxes, realizing that he was almost empty. He dropped the near empty guns and snatched a fresh one from its sling.

This time, he wasn't going to grandstand and waste ammunition like an amateur. Just because he had four hundred rounds of firepower didn't mean that it would find its target on automatic pilot. Both hands on the weapon, he stalked, keeping tight against the crates or anything that would stop a bullet.

Westerbridge didn't have the benefit of the smaller attacker's fleetness of foot and agility to dart between shelters from automatic fire. He poked slowly around one corner, spotting another gunman coming around the other way. The gangster's mind flashed quickly on the fact that this guy wasn't dressed in street clothes, and his face was smeared with black grease paint.

The massive gangster pulled the trigger a heartbeat before the man in black, pressing himself flat to the corner. A fireball from the front of the Ultimax burned like the inferno of hell just where he intended the mystery man to go.

THE EXECUTIONER HIT the ground as Sonny Westerbridge's torrent of machine-gun fire exploded. The big man may not have been able to beat Bolan in a footrace, but with his finger on the trigger, and at eight hundred rounds per minute, he had the advantage, Kevlar body armor or not, with the deadly weapon. Bolan rolled hard to keep out of sight and out of the way of the blistering fusillade.

From behind the sheltering concrete of a support column, Bolan weighed his options. The distance was too short for a 40 mm grenade to prime and explode. One of his conventional fragmentation grenades would likely take him out as well, if the shrapnel and shock wave weren't both deflected by the rows of shipping crates.

"You're gonna die, little man," Sonny Westerbridge said with a chuckle. "Your choice how—"

The Executioner wasn't a man who was afraid to die. Whether it was in the terrorist wars of the Middle East, stopping a Chinese spy plot threatening world peace, or just locked in battle with gangsters in Soho, he knew that one day his luck would run out, defending the weak and helpless on any scale. He wasn't, however, going to give up.

"Was that the same choice you gave Brenda Kightley, Westerbridge?" Bolan called out. This fight wasn't going to be won with mere bullets and brawn. The giant gangster was too savvy, too tough for a simple slug in the brain box.

"Kightley, Kightley… I don't remember no whore named Kightley, mate," Westerbridge answered. He was moving. Trying to home in on the Executioner's voice.

"An honest cop, ended her days with her head twisted 180 degrees, floating in Surrey Water," Bolan returned. He shifted his position after speaking, getting ten feet away from where he'd hidden. Neither man could see the other, though Bolan heard the indefinite scuffle of Westerbridge's heavy tread.

"Oh her. Fiery little minx… She really kicked when I gave her pretty little head a turn. You her partner? Naw, you're a Yank, and packing way too much firepower to be a London cop. Boyfriend?"

Bolan paused. The row he was heading toward was composed of cardboard boxes filled with contraband electronics. They'd provide some protection against a salvo of 5.56 mm military rounds, but hardly enough. Westerbridge was herding him toward a position of weakness. The Executioner cursed himself for not being fully aware of his battlefield. It was a small detail, but it could mean the difference between a crippled arm and full protection.

A minor, hairbreadth mistake could put him at a disadvantage in a serious, up close conflict. Bolan pulled one of his fragmentation grenades off his harness and cupped it gently. He rolled the mini-blaster on the floor, making sure it clattered and skittered on the hard concrete.

Westerbridge spotted it and bounced into view.

Bolan opened fire, but the big gangster's light beige suit only registered blackened tears as Parabellum rounds struck and were stopped by a layer of Kevlar. He went for a "failure drill," swinging from center of mass to the head, ripping off another burst, but the big man's skull and shoulders were back behind the protection of metal-skinned containers. Hollowpoint rounds sparked off steel, and the soldier stopped shooting.

The London giant was not going to be easy.

The Ultimax's barrel of the Ultimax poked around a corner, flaming, but Bolan was as well entrenched as Westerbridge. This would keep up until the law responded to the gunfire and explosions.

With his back to the hard concrete wall the warehouse's office stood on, Westerbridge was hard to approach.

Bolan's eyes narrowed, and he stuffed a new 40 mm shell into the breech of the grenade launcher. The stubby little M-576 round held scores of buckshot pellets, making the M-203 the equivalent of a sawed-off shotgun.

The Executioner stepped into the open, figuring his angles

like a pool player, and triggered the blast from the rifle-grenade launcher combo, spitting out pellets in a sizzling barrage at the concrete embankment at Westerbridge's back. The big gangster might have been unapproachable, but the swarm of round projectiles struck stone hard. Some embedded in the concrete, others bounced and sprayed back in a fan of peppering projectiles.

The gangster growled and grunted in rage and discomfort, stumbling into the open and spraying wildly. His pant leg on one side was soaked with blood, and his face was twisted into a mask of fury. Bolan felt two hammer blows strike him as he sidestepped. One round smashed his weapon from his fingers, plucking it from his hands and sending it hammering back into his chest. A second impact rolled off his vest-protected shoulder, the hit feeling like someone had dropped a small safe on his collarbone.

Westerbridge's Ultimax locked open empty, but Bolan could see that the man had a massive revolver holstered, and another light machine gun slung over his shoulder. Right arm numbed, Bolan was slow in grabbing for his Desert Eagle, his left hand instead twisting and plucking the Beretta from its shoulder holster, trying to outdraw the huge mobster.

But Westerbridge wasn't going for a fast draw. Instead, like a freight train, he lunged at Bolan, using the empty Ultimax like a spear and jarring Bolan's left forearm. The Italian machine pistol went flying from the Executioner's numbed fingers, but he managed to swing up his right fist, stuffed with the Desert Eagle, to jam it into Westerbridge's gut.

The wounded giant didn't even flinch from the impact, nor did he react to the first gunshot that exploded against his heavily muscled, Kevlar-wrapped side. Instead, massive arms slammed down on Bolan's shoulders, driving him to his knees with almost crippling force.

"I told you! I told you, but you didn't believe me!" Westerbridge shouted. "You're gonna get like that Kightley bitch, except I'm twisting your head all the fucking way off!"

Bolan hooked his right arm behind the giant's good leg and yanked back hard, punching the Englishman hard in the crotch. Westerbridge toppled backward, arms windmilling, fat, stubby fingers clawing at air and crates to keep from crashing to the floor. It was to no avail, and Bolan kept up the attack. Even as the British kingpin's foot left the floor, Bolan rolled forward. Using his own broad, muscular chest for leverage, he heaved with all the strength in his right arm on the big man's leg, hammering his left elbow with punishing force into Westerbridge's lower gut. The sound of a popping knee joint accompanied a strangled belch and the smell of vomit in the wake of the attack.

The Executioner lunged off Westerbridge's body, grabbing the Beretta and the Desert Eagle. His right arm still felt like limp spaghetti hanging from a battered shoulder, and his left forearm still tingled from the gangster's chop, but he twisted, aiming both cannons as Westerbridge was clawing for his revolver in its holster.

There was no contest this time in the fast draw. Bolan had the drop on Westerbridge and triggered both his handguns, only marginally recognizing the feeling of a heavy .44-caliber slug rolling across his ballistic-nylon protected ribs. The big man's head exploded. One lifeless blue eye stared at the ceiling, the other dangling from its socket from the impact of a .44 Magnum slug that had cratered his cheek.

The Executioner staggered to his feet, breathing hard. He shrugged his right shoulder, and from experience knew that it was only a minor injury, at worst a hairline fracture. He was certain that his left forearm was similarly bruised and battered from the way it tingled. Everything else, he could tell from a few twists of his torso, were mere bruises.

Bolan looked at the corpse at his feet, and frowned.

He wouldn't have much time to rest and mend.

There were plenty of murderers like Westerbridge in the world, and perhaps because the Executioner had waited too long to take his shot at the English kingpin, a cop was dead.

The howls of London's police cars reached his ears.

It was time to go.

2

Mack Bolan stopped at his war bag, sore and aching, but the first thing he did was pull out a bottle of antiseptic, no-rinse cleaning gel, and squeezed a healthy blob into the palm of his hand. Rubbing them together, then across his face and up into his hair, he smelled the rapidly evaporating alcohol content of the gel burning in his nostrils. After a few moments, his hands and face were dry, and the smell of gunpowder and blood on him was cut by half. He pulled out a packet of paper towels and gave himself another squeeze of the gel, and wiped the grime off his hands and face, so he wouldn't look like he'd just been engaged in a commando raid.

The approaching London police cars were small little boxes that the Executioner knew no American lawman would ever want to be driving around in. He stuffed the broken Colt SMG and its grenade launcher into his war bag, and covered himself up with a boot-length black duster that he had rolled up inside.

The Underground entrance at Brunel Road wasn't busy at that time of night, and dressed in black, with his collar flipped up, he didn't look so much like a badass as someone trying to dress too hip for his age group. Bolan wasn't interested in making the cover of *GQ,* though, so he didn't worry about what people thought of the big guy in a black turtleneck, the duster and boots. In fact, he encountered more than a couple of people who made him look positively tame, adorned in black leather and gleaming, reflective steel studs and body piercings.

He collapsed into a seat on the train and allowed himself to relax, rummaging a bottle of acetaminophen out of a side pocket of his bag and swallowing four of them dry. The ache in his bones subsided some as they came out from under the river and stopped at Wapping to take on and let off passengers. By the time he reached his stop, he was feeling refreshed and revitalized.

Getting up and out of the Underground system, he jogged north, stopping occasionally along the way to check for any tails.

There were no hunters in evidence, so Bolan pulled a bottle of water from his gear bag and took a sip, then continued walking toward the bed-and-breakfast where he'd rented a room.

Bolan passed a small synagogue and was crossing Nelson Street when a police car crawled around a corner. The soldier lowered his head and casually stepped into an alley without skipping a beat.

His shoulders tightened, instincts kicking into gear, footsteps softening to mere whispers as he gently put his weight on the balls of his feet. The war bag was lowered gently to the ground, the duster's front flap opening so that Bolan could reach the Beretta 93-R under his left arm.

He'd ducked into the alley to avoid police attention, and anything louder than the sound-suppressed Beretta would bring that weight down on him like a ton of bricks.

The Executioner had sworn an oath long ago—never to take the life of a lawman trying to do his job. He didn't think that would be a risk. London policemen were rarely armed, and any cops who did pack heat were members of the famous "Flying Squad." And by all reckoning, the Flying Squad would be back at Rotherhithe, all the way across the river, cleaning up the carnage of Westerbridge's shattered empire.

Danger was always present, though. He remembered that over the past couple months, there had been a series of murders in the area. Nothing recent enough to make the headlines, but enough to have still been the talk of the diner where Bolan had eaten.

Bolan disappeared into the shadows of the alley, the blunt nose of the suppressor leading the way.

What he stumbled upon was a scene out of madness. A woman lay on the glistening ground, her eyes still open, staring sightlessly. Her belly was slit from pubis to sternum, the sheets of abdominal muscle parted and rolled over the sides of her body like rubbery flats. Her stomach was emptied out, her intestines thrown over one shoulder, like a thick, rubbery boa. Bolan's jaw clenched as he watched the man over her finish scrawling, in blood, a cryptic phrase.

"The Juwes are not the men that will be blamed for nothing."

The man himself was an image out of a fever dream—a monstrosity ripped from a Victorian nightmare and made real. Draped in a long flowing cloak, the kind worn by period actors, and with a top hat adorning his head, he moved with an eerie swiftness and efficiency. He was tall and long-limbed, black gloves covering his big hands, and Bolan could have concealed a bazooka under the loose cloak the stranger wore. The Executioner wasn't a man given to cold fear, but surprise and shock washed over him.

The part of his mind that was the man, Mack Bolan, reeled, stunned by the combination of atrocity and the knowledge of a century of legend and mythology smacking him in the face. He half hoped that there was a movie camera nearby, that this was the filming of some movie. But the Executioner knew better.

There was no faking the stench of a disemboweled person, no faking the ugly swelling of a slashed throat. Not to someone who had seen similar atrocities in the basement abattoirs of Mafia turkey doctors.

The Executioner snapped up the Beretta and triggered a 3-round burst, catching the graffiti-writing murderer between the shoulder blades, smashing him facefirst into his own work, smearing some letters as he slumped down the wall. Shooting a man in the back didn't even register in Mack Bolan's mind.

There was no need for judge and jury in this case. The murderer was caught, literally red-handed. Bolan approached the two bodies, keeping the Beretta's muzzle aimed at the head of the unmoving figure.

Blank eyes stared at him from the dead woman, and once more, Bolan was reminded of the niggling anger he'd unleashed on Sonny Westerbridge. Perhaps if he'd arrived a few minutes earlier, those eyes would still see, instead of glaring sightlessly.

Bolan closed his eyes, trying to banish the thoughts. He was only human. He couldn't swoop down and save the world from itself.

Something rustled and Bolan snapped his attention to the figure of the Jack the Ripper imitator on the ground. He was twirling, leg lashing up and knocking the Beretta from his grasp with a bone-jarring impact.

Bolan lunged and grabbed the leg.

Unlike with Westerbridge, however, this fighter was prepared. He was already retrieving his limb from the Executioner's reach, one foot slamming into Bolan's ankle. Only the tough leather of his boot kept bone and muscle from being anything more than bruised by the kick, but it still took the soldier off his feet.

The Ripper rolled to his knees, sneering, his top hat fallen away to reveal a face obscured by black makeup across his eyes and cheeks. Bolan only had a glimpse of the face, before he returned his attention to protecting himself, lifting a forearm to block a second kick aimed for his head. The strike hurt like hell, but he didn't feel numbed paralysis in his fingers signaling a broken arm, and it was better than a skull fracture.

The Executioner lunged at the Ripper, shoulder cutting across the murderer at knee level and sending him toppling into the corpse of the murder victim. With all the strength he could muster, Bolan swung a fist toward the head of the murderer, but the cloaked killer lifted his shoulder and blocked the blow with a solid knob of muscular flesh and bone. The Ripper hooked his hand over Bolan's forearm and pulled back hard, drawing a knife into the fight. Bolan raised his other forearm, catching his adversary across his wrist, blocking a lethal downward stab.

This wasn't the blade of Jack the Ripper. It was a Gerber Light Military Fighter, six inches of razor-sharp, stainless steel with a decidedly modern glass-injected, nylon handle. Either way, it was sharp, it was pointy, and if Bolan slipped, he would be heartbeats away from being carved into thin slices.

The two men struggled against each other, the Executioner off balance, but his back and legs holding him up against the splayed-out but aggressive Ripper. They held that pose, a long tense moment, muscles straining, breaths creaking from closed-off throats, sweat soaking down through matted hair. It was a fight that would go on until they both suddenly gave out, muscles collapsing, and in that moment, the killer would have the slight edge. It was do or die, so Bolan let himself be folded under the pressure.

The Executioner rolled with the momentum of his opponent's pull, dropping himself farther out of the knife's slicing arc, and allowing himself the leverage to bring both boots up and rocketing into the Ripper's knife-arm and chest. The impact jarred them both apart, separating them and giving Bolan breathing space to somersault back and go for his Desert Eagle.

So much for stealth. Bolan knew the Ripper had to be wearing some kind of armor, armor that needed more penetration than the Beretta's hollowpoint rounds could provide. Even if he brought down half of the London Police Force and a regiment of SAS troops, this dangerous psychotic needed to be taken out of action, and that meant only the special kind of bone-shattering force that a 240-grain hollowpoint round could provide.

He triggered the big pistol, and the Ripper leaped for cover, his cloak obscuring the outline of his head. The fact that he was still moving meant that Bolan's snap-shot missed. The Ripper's dash continued, his head and body obscured by the cloak, making it almost impossible to determine where to shoot for a solid stop.

For the second time that night, Bolan offered up a grudging helping of respect for an opponent. This man may have proved a mentally unstable slasher, but he was also a formidable combatant. The Executioner chased him with three more .44 Magnum slugs in rapid succession, but between his armor and his speed, the Ripper reached the shielding bulk of a trash Dumpster, Bolan's last two shots hammering steel instead of flesh.

The soldier took the brief pause to reload his Desert Eagle when the flashing outline of the cloak whipped around the corner of the garbage container. He triggered a fresh slug into the shadowy mass, and was answered with the sudden flare of a muzzle-flash. Impacts hammered along the Executioner's chest, knocking him back on his heels, and Bolan fell to the ground, burning pain searing across his ribs.

The killer stepped out into the open, leveling the boxy frame of an Uzi- or Ingram-style machine pistol at Bolan's fallen form. He inched closer, keeping the muzzle aimed at the downed warrior, then cursed, looking both ways up and down the alley.

"R-1, R-1, report," came the crackle of a radio from inside the folds of the Ripper's cloak.

"I've encountered resistance, I had to take action," the killer answered. "Christ! I need help cleaning up this shit."

"What do you mean?"

"What do I mean? This bloke comes out of nowhere and shoots me in the back. Next thing I know, a perfectly good serial killer scene is sporting enough brass from automatic weapons to start a fucking band!"

"Who was he?" the radio called.

"How the fuck should I know? We'll run his face and prints after we dump him," the Ripper replied.

"Dump him?"

"Of course dump him, you idiots," the killer snapped. "What, we're supposed to have the police believe that someone pulled an imitation of Jack the Ripper, and then, in the same alley in the same night, a heavily armed commando-type gets shot to death?"

"We've been yanking their chains for years, Ripper One."

"Just get here and help me out."

"We're on our way, hold your ground," came the answer over the communicator.

Ripper One stepped even closer, kicking the Desert Eagle out of Bolan's limp fingers. The massive handgun clattered down the alley, and the murderer stepped back, flexing his grip on the handle of his MAC-11. Since the Executioner was down, he popped the empty clip and fed it a fresh one, never letting the muzzle sway from the motionless soldier. If there was any life in him, he'd have at least one shot to put things right if the man moved in mid-reload.

"You were pretty heavily armed for a short jaunt tonight, eh? A machine pistol and that fucking bazooka... I'll be sporting bruises for a month. I wonder who you are?"

Ripper One tapped his toe into Bolan's ribs, looking for any response. The man in black didn't move in response to the kick. The Ripper realized that Bolan had only barely fallen for the oldest trick in the book, and only after a fight that left him battered and bruised. He wasn't going to make the same mistake that the Executioner had and let his attention wander from a fallen foe.

At least not until he heard the scrunch of wheels at the close end of the alley.

"It's about time," the Ripper said, looking over his shoulder.

I agree, the Executioner thought, still feigning death.

Bolan was waiting to make a move the moment the killer dropped his guard, but so far the man was a by-the-book professional. Only a reluctance to have to police more bullet casings on his otherwise "pristine" murder scene had kept the madman from pulling the trigger and splattering Bolan's brains all over the alley. But a gory head shot would have made even more of a mess of bloody evidence that wouldn't match.

Whoever this guy was, he was obsessive about maintaining an image. Obsessive to the point that he might be in fear for his life if his ruse was blown by the slightest misstep.

The stench of a cover-up overwhelmed the stink of gore and gunpowder in the alley.

Bolan's arm was starting to fall asleep, folded under his back, the steel frame of the Beretta poking him in the back and making him ache all the more. Falling on the gun was like taking a massive stapler to his spine, and his arm felt like it was going to pop from its socket.

But it was better than the pain of having his lungs collapse if the Ripper's bullets had gotten through Bolan's Kevlar vest—and it made him look like a convincing corpse.

The Ripper and his friends surrounded Bolan, three of them in total, and they bent to hook his shoulders and his feet. The Executioner's gun hand dangled, Beretta still fisted. He fired point-blank into the foot of one man, his 9 mm slug smashing through leather, flesh and bone, raising a howl of agony.

Curses of fright filled the air and Bolan exploded into action, firing at the Ripper at crotch level. The killer managed to back off and reach for his own machine pistol.

Bolan had registered that his enemies had almost full-torso protection on their armor, even having a groin tabard. A pelvic hit would have dropped a man instantly thanks to the vulnerable bones and blood vessels at that intersection of the body. The Executioner fired a second burst at the Ripper to discourage him, then swung his weapon toward the man over his shoulder. A kick lashed out to disarm him again, but Bolan rolled out of the way. He was sick of being left weaponless this night. To express his displeasure at the subsequent effort, he fired a burst that tore out the thigh of the attacker.

Another man appeared from the van, aiming a weapon that outclassed the machine pistols and handguns at play in the alley—a Belgian Minimi-SAW. The weapon had two hundred rounds and was meant for use against vehicles, large concentrations of enemy troops, and as a force multiplier for small units against larger forces, much like the Ultimax that had nearly claimed Bolan's life only an hour earlier.

Unlike Sonny Westerbridge, this guy knew how to lay down suppressive fire with a squad automatic weapon, dividing the alley between the Executioner and his opponents. The gunner was good, creating a wall of flying lead that would prove lethal to Bolan should he try to attack the Ripper and his crew, but stopped short of harming the trio. Bolan dived for cover behind a Dumpster as the storm of autofire hammered at him. Even the rolled steel shell of the container didn't stop some of the slugs and bullets whizzed through perforated steel. The Ripper limped rapidly past him, and Bolan aimed for his head, triggering a 9 mm slug, but was driven back under cover by the rain of doom from the vehicle.

"Go! Go! Go!" the Ripper shouted.

Bolan made mental notes about the mysterious killer. Full-torso body armor, communications, unmarked transport and a machine gunner whose skill with a light machine gun rivaled his own—this guy was no simple madman.

The Ripper came back for his men, hauling them along while the gunner in the van continued his rock-and-roll serenade. He pushed his companions into the side door of the van, a black Volkswagen. The Executioner swung around, firing the Beretta until it ran dry, but the vehicle tore off, wheels screaming like a ghost, disappearing into the streets of Whitechapel.

Bolan raced to catch a sign of the van, but it whirled out of sight.

Breathless, exhausted, covered with more injuries, Bolan contemplated the deadly mix of horrific history and decidedly modern technology.

Bolan glanced back to the lifeless form of the woman, defeat weighing him down as much as exhaustion.

Brass casings surrounded her, like a halo of golden tears flickering in the half-light spilling off the street. Her blue eyes met his, one final question in them, maybe even an answer that she would know, but could not tell anymore, an answer that would only come to light by finding her murderers.

He pulled out the small digital camera he kept in his pocket, a flat, bleeding-edge piece of technology that would allow him to take photographs of evidence he'd stumble across in the course of his battles. He got a picture of the victim's face, though not quite sure what he'd do with it. Maybe Aaron Kurtzman back at Stony Man Farm could run the image, give him a head start on investigating the woman's past and figure out why an armed commando team would dress as the Jack the Ripper and murder her in Whitechapel.

The weary soldier retrieved his Desert Eagle and his war bag, and limped off toward his room.

He was going to have to get as much rest as he could before morning because he was going to bring judgment to Jack the Ripper.

3

Liam Tern rubbed his chest, feeling the sore spots where two .44 Magnum slugs had connected solidly with his rib cage, hammering him even through the Kevlar body armor he wore. Suddenly, he was glad to have been wearing the heavy vestments of his Jack the Ripper disguise. Its flapping folds had obscured his body, throwing off the shooter's point of aim.

"How are Danny and Serge?" he asked, entering the improvised sick bay.

"Serge looks like he's gonna lose his leg. Danny's foot is a hell of a mess," the old man said, stripping off his rubber gloves. He hobbled over to the sink and Tern glanced over to Serge, who was in a doped-out state on the table. His leg had been torn apart by a point-blank burst of autofire, the muscle shredded away to expose gleaming white bone, shattered by a single 9 mm slug.

Danny was sitting in the corner, looking at the table, his face gaunt, his eyes wide with fear. "If Serge is going to lose that leg—"

Tern shook his head.

"Take it easy, Danny. He'll be looked after," Tern cooed in reassurance. He smiled gently at the young man, giving his brush-short red hair a tousle.

Tern glanced back at the old man, who shrugged and turned his back.

The blade's handle was in Tern's palm, but the wounded young man heard the sound of para cord striking the professional's grip. Danny's forearm bore down hard across Tern's, his hazel eyes going wide, seeing betrayal.

"You fucking liar!" the kid bellowed.

Tern swept his hand down into Danny's face, plunging his thumb into his eye. There was a grunt and a grimace, but the youngest member of the Ripper crew wasn't letting go. The kid wasn't distracted by the attack. An eye gouge wasn't like getting a belly full of steel. Tern didn't blame the kid as he pushed to get his knife up and into Danny's gut.

"Just relax and die, Danny," Tern snarled.

"Oh for God's sake," the old man grumbled.

Danny's forehead suddenly exploded, blood spraying across Tern's features, stinging his eyes. Hazel eyes stared sightlessly, head lolling on the shoulders of the dead man.

Tern dumped Danny on the table against the wall and turned just in time to see the old man level his pistol and put a mercy shot into Serge's forehead. Serge jerked with the single impact, then was still. He couldn't feel any more pain.

The old man unscrewed the sound suppressor from his pistol and plopped it in his pocket, holstering the gun.

"De Simmones…" Tern began.

"Lift with your knees, not your back," the old man said with a wink. "We'll dispose of them later."

Tern sighed and shoved his shoulder under Danny's sternum, lifting him up and flopping him onto Serge's corpse.

He regretted having to kill Danny and Serge. Having two injured men would have alerted the authorities. A man with a leg broken by a point-blank burst of submachine-gun fire would have made any hospital suspicious. Serge would have bled to death in the amount of time it would have taken to find a physician with the skill and facilities to save his life. The man's bleeding and the loss of the limb were his doom anyway.

Danny, on the other hand, was an even greater risk. He hadn't been prepared for resistance, and getting shot gave Tern an expectation of what the kid was going to be like. He'd signed onto the job easy enough, having cut his way through the ranks, proving his toughness against the untrained shit-kickers in Ireland.

It was one thing to handle disorganized protesters and terrorists who were more successful at blowing themselves up with their own bombs. Against a fighting man like the soldier they'd just faced, Tern had realized Danny folded. He'd seen a killing machine whirling in action. Two of them, when Tern counted himself. The display had unseated Danny. In the future, there would have been too much of a pause, that niggling panic waiting to flare up and slow down the young fighter.

Tern rolled Danny's eyelids closed then wrapped both of the dead bodies in plastic tarp.

"De Simmones said you needed help," Carlton said as he entered the room. He was much shorter than Tern, only five foot six, but his upper body was thick and broad. Forearm muscles were laid in thick, rippling sheets poking out from under rolled-up sleeves, and he hefted one end of the tarp-wrapped body pack as easily as he handled the monstrous recoil of a machine gun.

"Makes you wonder what'll happen when it's our time," Tern said.

Carlton shrugged his blocky shoulders. "We may get lucky and go out fast. Frankly, I always save a bullet for myself, so I don't end up suffering like Serge."

Tern shook his head. Serge had been a member of their team for a while. He was a vetted, blooded soldier. Unlike Danny, Serge had been hardened against tough odds.

As depressing as it was for the new kid to turn out to be a failure, it was worse when a longtime partner was dropped, and so easily.

No, it wasn't easy.

The man in black was a damned good fighter. And Serge's mangled leg was the source of agony. Tern still felt the bruises on his forearm where his fingers had dug in.

Tern took the other end of the tarp and they carried it to the van. "We'll take the bodies to an incinerator."

Carlton nodded as he backed into the van, the doors being held open by De Simmones and Courtley, the driver.

Tern glanced at De Simmones who just smiled. The smile said everything that Tern suspected. He and his men were expendable, and De Simmones wasn't afraid to put a bullet into any of their heads.

"Come on, we have a long day ahead of us," De Simmones replied.

"What about the man in black?" Carlton asked.

"I've called up Ripper Two for this job," Tern told him. "If there's anything left of him when they're done with him, we'll get called in for the kill."

"Right now, we need distance," De Simmones stated. "We're an organization. Let's take advantage of our strength in numbers, all right?"

Tern smirked.

He was glad, for now, that he was counted as a useful number. He still intended to keep his guns close in case that ledger ever changed against him.

HAL BROGNOLA KNEW the mathematics of asset versus risk that Mack Bolan provided to the Stony Man Farm project. While he was a useful member in the program to keep America safe from threats foreign and domestic, there was also a factor of risk whenever the Executioner was involved.

At that moment, the only mental math he wanted to do was to add five hours to the time to figure out where his longtime friend was while he was stuck in the Farm's War Room, keeping a close eye on a Phoenix Force mission.

"It's almost six there, isn't it?" Brognola asked.

"That's right," Bolan answered. "You're burning the midnight oil."

"What's this about?" Brognola asked.

"I was on the way back to my place when I came on a murder scene, and the murderer," Bolan explained. "He was wearing body armor and packing a machine pistol. And he is good."

"'Is,' as in still running around?" Brognola inquired.

"Still driving around, with a van full of automatic weapons, two injured coworkers, and one of the best machine gunners I've ever run across," Bolan said. "I've been cleaning up injuries from that fight for the past couple hours."

"All this to murder some woman in…" Brognola began. "Whitechapel?"

"Yeah. The killer was dressed up as Jack the Ripper."

"You're joking with me, right?"

"Have I ever yanked your chain before, Hal?"

"Jack the Ripper–style killing, in Whitechapel, with a machine gunner for backup?"

Bolan grunted in affirmation. "At the very least. He had two more and a driver. But one suffered some severe injuries. He might not make it."

Brognola picked up his coffee mug. "Nothing major is going on here that you have to attend to. It sounds like you should stay and see what's behind this murder."

"Thanks, Hal. Think you can get me some authorization?"

"For what?"

"I want to work with the local Ripper task force."

"You think this guy's been doing this for a while?" Brognola asked.

"I did some research. I ran across references to Ripperstyle murders, and there have been nine in the past three years."

"Any solved?"

"Only one. Scotland Yard couldn't link the other eight to the guy they caught, so they think he was just a copycat," Bolan answered. "I'm not much of a gambler, but I'm betting there was a very definite pattern on mutilation going on." Bolan described the murder scene he'd stumbled across.

"The intestines were thrown over the right shoulder, just as in the original Ripper murders? Wasn't that an execution according to Masonic ritual?" Brognola asked.

"No. When the Masons executed their victims, they removed the heart and threw it over the *left* shoulder," Bolan answered. "There's a belief that the 'Juwes' graffiti was meant to throw authorities off the trail."

"I'll make some calls to Scotland Yard," Brognola said. "Maybe I can get you in on the investigation."

"Even if I only touch base with them for a few hours, it'll still give me some leads to go on. If I can't, then I'll do some bouncing around the underworld. Someone had to supply those guys with their hardware. Machine pistols might be easy to sell, but I took out one major dealer who sold squad automatic weapons. There can't be many of those in England, let alone London."

"Striker, just be careful. I'll call you later. Get some rest, okay?" Brognola said.

"I'll try," Bolan answered over the phone link, before it died.

THE SUN'S RISING did nothing to lighten Inspector Melissa Dean's mood as she got out of her car. Officers were surrounding the alley, and she had passed by the other street. It was cut off on both ends, the flickering lights atop police vehicles splashing the slick streets with reds and blues. She walked closer, knowing from the call what to expect.

It still wasn't a pretty smell, the stench of a gutted body yet fresh in the air.

It also smelled like the aftermath of a fireworks display. She bent and picked up a piece of brass, rolling it between her fingertips. The bottom had no stamp of caliber or maker, let alone a lot number, and she frowned. From the look of it, it was a simple 9 mm case. She'd seen enough of them working homicide, but none so clean.

There was a polite cough and she looked up to see a tall Asian man standing nearby. She recognized his pale, round face instantly, his long black hair flowing in the wind.

Kevin Goh managed a weak smile as he walked over to her, holding a plastic evidence bag full of similar brass casings. On the ground, white tape marked where each cartridge had been found. More tape marks were on the walls, pointing out bullet impacts.

Dean started to count them as Goh walked with her, but the number of holes and casings was enormous.

"Sorry to ring you up so early," Goh said, shrugging against the cold.

"A Ripper-style murder and a gunfight?" Dean asked, looking around.

"Yeah. At the other end of the alley, there's disintegrating belt links as well as rifle ammunition. NATO caliber."

"In English for those of us who don't speak gun," Dean said.

Goh smirked. "Someone used a full-blown machine gun, as well as at least three other weapons here last night."

"Three weapons?"

"A pistol. And two different kinds of submachine gun. One was firing 9 mm shorts. One was firing 9 mm Luger rounds. And the pistol was a Magnum autoloader."

Dean shook her head, running her fingers through her short blond hair. "Magnum."

"Forty-four to be exact," Goh told her.

Dean pursed her lips. "Someone with a Dirty Harry complex?"

"Someone took a big bite out of Sonny Westerbridge's skull last night. And .44 Magnum and 9 mm machine pistol ammunition mixed in with what Sonny's men had," Goh replied. He plucked the casing from her fingertips and showed her the blank end stamp. "The Magnums were also unmarked."

"But Sonny's usually based out of Rotherhithe," Dean said.

"Not anymore. He and nearly forty-five of his men are dead. Gunfire, explosions and one knifing."

Dean shook her head. "I'm sure the knife job wasn't like this."

Not if it's like our usual boy, she added mentally.

Goh looked at her for a moment, and Dean realized that the Asian detective was a recent addition to London's finest. Homicides West, East and South, as well as the Serious and Organized Crime unit, were familiar with a pattern, over the years, of criminals and terrorists who came to brutal ends.

There were rumors that these were covert SAS operations, or even the work of men from overseas. When the homicide teams tried to come up with a clue, they were usually stonewalled. The stonewalling was frustrating, but since the victims were thugs and murderers themselves, the police reluctantly dropped the cases. One of these common links was the blank ammunition, and the predominant calibers used. Forty-four Magnum and 9 mm Luger.

They never had much more on this mystery force except that it was small, efficient and rarely brought harm to any bystanders. Dean decided to keep quiet about this, but she couldn't help wonder if the death of Westerbridge and his men were related to this alley fight in any way other than the mystery fighter.

"Two sides shooting at each other and using the same kind

of phantom ammo," Dean said. "Any information on the victim?"

"No bullet holes in her, except for what looked like an old scar on a flap of her stomach," Goh told her.

Dean walked toward the body, Goh on her heels. She knelt before the dead woman. The body had been disturbed, half pushed onto its side, probably by fighters bumping into her. The grime on the floor of the alley was scuffed with boot marks where big, heavy men had battled.

"Are we done taking pictures of the body?"

Goh nodded toward the crime-scene photographers. "They'll be taking her to forensics in a few minutes."

Dean sighed. "I'll look around here and try to get a feel for the crime scene."

Goh tilted his head. "You seem to have a feeling already, Melissa."

Dean swept the alley, drifting off for a moment, looking at the pockmarks from weapons, smelling the stink of urban warfare and serial murder all sewn up into a tiny corridor of stone and garbage. It was a claustrophobic place where men had tried to kill each other, and one presumably innocent woman lost her life.

The vibes given by the scene were strange.

If enigmas had a scent, Melissa Dean now knew how to recognize it.

Sometimes, if you've been to enough murder scenes, you developed a taste for what it was all about. Some were madness. Some were fury. Fueled by jealousy, betrayal, loneliness—she'd had felt them all.

This was different. There was no emotion in this.

The body was too perfectly filleted, too neatly placed. Just how the other Ripper kills were set up.

But the addition of Westerbridge's killer…that was a new twist.

How could it not be? The kind of firepower used doesn't show up more than once a year in London's back streets, she thought. Now twice in one night?

There's no such thing as coincidence.

Dean shook her head. "Where are you heading now?"

"Back to the station. Need a lift?" Goh offered.

"I have my own wheels," Dean replied. "But I'll meet you there."

The mental images of two horrors, one a century and a half old, and one thoroughly modern formed an amorphous blob of murder and mayhem in the middle of the city she was sworn to protect. The burden hung on her, troubling her on the drive back.

4

Try as he might to put aside his theories and memories about the previous night's murder, Mack Bolan couldn't shake them. But he wasn't completely left cold.

As he showed up at the offices of London's Metropolitan Police Homicide East unit, the Executioner felt the usual tingle he felt whenever he entered a police station while on a mission. Hal Brognola had arranged credentials that were so far above reproach they could bounce a small nuclear warhead. But none of that gave Bolan the impression that he was truly safe. The gulf that stood between the lone soldier and the forces of law enforcement was one that was hard to cross without the sense that he was walking a tightrope.

There were just too many variables for him to truly feel comfortable working inside a system—the possibility of dealing with corruption, of losing brave allies, of being too constrained by the rules and allowing his enemy to slip away to cost more lives…

Bolan took a deep breath. He had no patience for those who got away, literally, with murder. And so, he spoke to those killers in their own bloody language—regardless of laws.

He reached the watch commander, a sturdily built, square-shouldered, full-faced woman with long, once black hair shot through with streaks of silver. She was in her fifties, no longer the fresh-faced youthful beauty she had once been, but something shined through the crow's-feet and smile lines. She had a sharp eye as keen and hardened as any beat cop. She looked down on him with a matronly glower.

"Can I help you, sir?" she asked.

"I'm here to see Detectives Dean and Goh, Homicide East."

She pursed her full lips, studying him for a moment, disapproval crossing her face. She cleared her throat. "Their desks are on the second floor, in the Homicide East squad room. They're expecting you, Detective Cooper."

"Thank you," Bolan replied.

He followed the desk sergeant's directions and was soon at the desk of an unlikely couple of lawmen sitting at face-to-face desks, paperwork and foam cups littering them, computer screens displaying crime scene reports.

Goh looked up at Bolan, dark eyes taking him in with a single glance as his raven hair fell in sheets off his collar.

Dean had short blond hair that stopped at her collar and piercing, pale blue eyes that almost mirrored his own. She studied him as well, her gaze penetrating, trying to cut through the layers of pretense he was hiding behind. While Goh was offering his hand in greeting, she was holding back, tense and withdrawn, in observer mode.

Bolan took Goh's hand.

"Matt Cooper," Bolan offered.

"Kevin Goh." The detective's flawless East End accent indicated he was London born and raised, or at least raised. His grip was strong and firm. "This is Melissa Dean."

"Pleasure," she said, but making no effort to act like it was.

"Likewise," he answered. He was sincere about it, but wondered how far behind he was on his rapport with these two.

"So you're interested in the latest run of Ripper killings?" Goh asked.

"Yeah. I was interested in the case. Meredith Jones-Jakes,

about five months ago, was the last one I'd heard about," Bolan explained. "Then this morning, there was supposedly another one?"

"You seem to have learned about it pretty quickly," Dean spoke up in a stinging broadside. "Coincidence?"

He met her gaze unflinchingly. "There's no such thing as coincidence."

"So what are you doing so far from the colonies?" Dean pressed.

"You have the paperwork sitting on your desk."

Dean pushed it aside. "Administrative leave from the Boston Police Department. That's the reason. What's the story?"

"I'm set to testify in three months," Bolan told her. "And I'm under a gag order about anything else."

Dean's eyes narrowed. "A mobster?"

"Make of it what you will."

"That's why you're traipsing through a Met station packing a hand cannon under your jacket? The Mafia doesn't have roving hit squads around the world, Detective."

Bolan was tempted, for half a heartbeat, to tell her that she was wrong. Early on in his career, he'd run into more than enough heavily armed gangsters in Soho, giving him his first experiences with the awesome Weatherby Mark V and the efficient Uzi 9 mm submachine gun. And only a few hours previously, he could have shocked her with the level of hardware at Sonny Westerbridge's Rotherhithe warehouse.

Instead, Bolan remained diplomatic. "It's not a cannon. And it's cleared."

Dean's jaw set firmly. "I just don't want to see it unless we come under fire from the entire Peruvian Third Naval Commando unit, all right?"

Bolan took a notebook and pen from the pocket of his gray windbreaker. "Is that only the Peruvian Third Naval Commando unit, or is that indicative of the level of opposition?"

Dean sighed heavily. "We're going to check out the body at the morgue, smart-ass. Are you going to join us, or are you going to try and join the cast of *Dead Ringers*?"

"Melissa, as much as I'd love to see you get into a catfight, I think you'd have to have it with a woman," Goh said. "I'm sorry, Detective Cooper. She's not usually like this."

Bolan looked Dean over. "I'm not offended. If a foreigner was going to step into one of my cases, I'd be uptight too."

Dean stood, grabbing her brown leather jacket, flipping it around her slender shoulders. Hard eyes met his. "Uptight? Try suspicious."

The Executioner watched her as she was leaving the squad room. She stopped halfway to the door and glared back at Goh and him. "Are you two coming?"

Bolan looked to Goh, who could only shrug. "We're coming, Melissa."

The two men followed the detective.

As THE IRATE Vincent Black strode to his car, his two men fell into step behind him. He spent a moment checking the .50-caliber Desert Eagle he had in a shoulder holster, then waited for Sal to open his door while Tony stepped around to the driver's side.

Black ducked his head and got into the back seat.

The old man was a pain in his ass, calling him out on jobs whenever he felt like it, but in a way, that pain helped Black along.

After all, Black was in the business of hurting people.

And he was good at it.

"Just watch whoever's going into the Met today," De Simmones told him. "We're looking for a tall man, six-three. Black hair, blue eyes. Someone who looks hard and business-like."

Black settled in comfortably for the surveillance. Being

caught with an unlicensed handgun right in front of the police station would land him in more trouble than he was willing to pay his lawyers to get him out of. He shrugged, flattened his coat lapel with the palm of one hand, and watched from across the street.

It wasn't long before the man matching the description De Simmones had given him drove into a parking garage next to the police station, then headed inside. Black checked the guy out.

He was big, but he was lean and proportional, moving with the facile grace of a panther. He also had confidence, layered under an alertness not based on paranoia, but on the kind of awareness you only got when you walked into some hard places nobody expected you to walk out of.

Black could identify with the guy. He'd been in a lot of traps, and he bore the knife scars and more than a couple of circular bullet scars from close encounters with men who had tried to be as bad as he was.

Black still walked. They didn't. Some of them didn't even smell fresh air anymore.

I'd like to see this big bloke in action, he thought. And when it's all over, I'll put a single .50-caliber slug into the middle of the stranger's face and blow out his brains.

THOUGH HE COULD HARDLY be considered squeamish, the Executioner rarely went to a morgue. He rarely needed to, and he had seen enough of the people he loved and respected laid out under cold white sheets on flat metal tables. Too many soldiers on the same side, too many beloved, too many family members, all cold and on a slab, never to move again. Posing as a detective, though, he had no choice.

Bolan looked at the familiar face, staring up. Her eyes were still open, and he was tempted to ask why they had been left that way, but he knew particulate matter sometimes showed up on the cornea, which would provide some clues as to who killed her or how she died. It was often the little details solved a mystery. Sometimes looking into the eyes of a dead woman could give a moment of insight into her murder.

He was leaning over her, examining her more closely when the medical examiner, a balding man with a hooked nose and gunmetal gray hair, cleared his throat.

"Are you in any way a forensic technician, Detective Cooper?" the ME asked.

Bolan shook his head.

"Then kindly piss off." The irate glower dissolved into a friendly wink. Bolan snorted, an abortive laugh in these dreary, desolate surroundings, but at least it was a moment of wry humor on the part of the examiner. "I'm Dr. Felix Randman."

"Matt Cooper."

"From New Hampshire, aren't you?"

"You're pretty good at catching accents," Bolan said. However, for the purposes of his charade, for the purpose of working with the local British homicide cops, he was reverting to how he spoke when he grew up in Pittsfield, Massachusetts. For a long time, he had sublimated his accent, having learned to speak with a more anonymous tone, akin to the voice that the network news anchors called "Midwest neutral."

"I spent a year at MGH," Randman stated. He came around the table and looked down into the dead girl's eyes.

Bolan looked serious. "One of the first graduates?" he asked.

Randman glanced up at Bolan, then grinned at the soldier. "You give as good as you get."

"What's that mean?" Dean asked.

"Massachusetts General Hospital is the third oldest hospital in North America," Randman explained.

"So he called you a dried-up old fart?" Dean asked.

Randman narrowed his eyes at her. "Yes."

"I may like you yet, Cooper," she said with a hint of approval.

Bolan nodded. "Now that we've broken the ice, you were going to show us something about her eyes?"

"Yes. They were dilated prior to her demise. She was in a drugged state," Randman said.

"Well, the insides of her thighs were a mass of track marks, according to your report," Goh spoke up.

"Small problem. All the track marks were clean and uniform and about the same level of scarring, meaning they were almost the same age," Randman explained.

"Was this the same as with the other women?" Bolan asked.

"You catch on quickly."

"Someone wanted it to look like these girls were just off the street, full of smack and doing their tours," Dean said, walking around.

"On top of that, she has none of the long-term effects of heroin abuse," Randman stated. "Her legs show a lot of track marks. But she has no collapsed veins, no signs of bacterial infections or abscesses. The heart looks perfectly fine, uninfected and no damage to the valve or the lining. I'm betting that once I saw her skull open, I'm not going to find any neurological trauma."

Bolan frowned. "And what is that circular scar on her stomach, just poking out of her navel, see it?"

Dean and Goh looked for it. Randman pointed it out with the tip of a probe. "You've got sharp eyes, Cooper."

"It looks like someone performed laproscopic surgery on her," Randman stated. "Something was inserted."

"And that someone took it back," Bolan answered. "The whole Ripper reenactment would just be a smoke screen."

"It wouldn't be the first time," Goh answered. "Some his-

torians believe that the Ripper murders weren't so much a serial killer at work, but someone covering up a conspiracy."

"There's that," Bolan replied. "William Gull was supposed
to be the man responsible for hunting down and killing the
five women who knew about Edward's fathering a bastard
child."

"There is a problem with that theory, if you might recall,"
Dean spoke up.

"You mean that whole thing with Gull being in his eight-
ies, having suffered a stroke and a heart attack, and eviscerating his victims in a cab running through the middle of a
crowded London neighborhood?" the Executioner asked.

"That's the one," Dean answered.

"No plan is perfect. But whatever went on, it certainly
stirred up enough controversy over an entire century to keep
the waters muddied," Bolan said.

Goh shook his head. "So what was inserted into her?"

Randman shrugged. "I ran some X-rays to see if I could
get an impression from what was left behind. When a knife
is used against flesh or any other soft target, it leaves behind
trace elements of metal. I have wear patterns and was hoping to find some trace of what was inserted into our poor girl."

"How soon will it be done?" Dean asked.

"They've been having problems with the X-rays on her,"
Randman stated. "The last shot of her was overexposed.
We're trying to fix the glitch now, and we're not exactly on
the priority to take her to the main hospital's Radiology
department."

"Why's that?" Bolan asked.

Randman looked crestfallen as he felt the sting in Bolan's
voice. "Because, Detective Cooper, even if she is the latest
to bear the mark of Jack the Ripper's rampage across the
centuries, is not important. We don't even have an identity
for her."

"Jane Doe. Another victim left to fall to the wayside because she isn't strong or important enough, right?"

"That's the way it goes, Detective. I don't like it, but that's the way it goes. It's not a perfect world, and justice isn't always done," Randman stated.

"It may not be a perfect world, but I can sure as hell try for some justice," Bolan replied.

AS SOON AS THE MAN in black went into the ME's office, Vincent Black got out of the back seat of his car. Tony and Sal braced him on either side, obscuring him from casual observers on the street. In the trunk was a trio of sawed-off shotguns, blasters no longer than two feet. They kicked like hell, but they each held four shots, with one in the breech. They had enough firepower to take on any opposition short of encountering a small platoon of Bosnian guerrillas on an ethnic cleansing spree. If that wasn't enough, Black had his Desert Eagle, and Sal and Tony were packing 9 mm Glocks.

However, if it got to that point, Black wasn't going to be standing his ground and fighting. Since 9/11, the metropolitan police were very quick to respond to potential terrorist activities. The armed response vehicle units were descended from the legendary Flying Squad—the lawmen who were charged to the task of responding to armed violence with their own force of arms. The Firearms Unit was ranked among the best in Europe, and was equipped with some of the best technology and armor in any police force's arsenal. If the ARV wasn't enough, then the cops would call in the Anti-Terrorist Branch, SO13, who could bring anything up to sniper rifles into a heated siege.

Black figured the hit on big Sonny Westerbridge the night before had only gone off so completely because his warehouse was in a fairly secluded area of the docks and it was at a time of night when anyone there was staying close to heavy machinery and keeping to themselves. The London button man paused for a moment as he slipped the sawed-off scattergun under his trench coat.

De Simmones was asking him to take out this mystery stranger on the heels of Westerbridge's snuffing it. There was something unsettling about the tall American. Not that Black could put his finger on it, but he was a familiar type. When someone like him appeared, some big, bad people disappeared.

Often in the middle of violent firefights.

"Something wrong, boss?" Sal asked.

"Keep your head about you," Black told his man. "The guy we're gunning for isn't going to be an easy mark."

"There's three of us, and even if he is armed, the two bobbies with him aren't," Tony spoke up.

"That's a pretty little delusion, but I don't get told to go after someone because they're an easy mark," Black grumbled.

"You're being a little paranoid," Sal suggested.

Black took a handful of Sal's collar. "Then you can sit in the bloody car and keep the engine running."

Sal swallowed. Vincent Black was six-four and two hundred pounds of lean, hard muscle. He was all sharp edges and hard corners. His shoulders were broad and square, his chest a triangle that disappeared into a thirty-two-inch waistband. Dressed in black with ironed seams that were as sharp as razor blades, he looked like something that would put a man's eye out. The only thing blunt about Black was his manner with people.

Blunt and straight to the point.

"Whatever you want, boss," Sal said.

"I want you to get your head out of your ass."

Sal nodded. "Sure, Vinnie."

"And I want three shotgun muzzles aimed at that piece of shit the moment he comes out that door."

Sal nodded even more emphatically. "All you had to do was ask."

Black smirked. His mouth was a cruel thing that split his craggy, carved features. "Let's go."

Tucking the guns deep under their jackets, the three men crossed the street. Sal and Tony walked, following Black, only a foot behind him, close enough to let him know that they were there, far enough to give him room to move. Cars stopped. Only one driver had the temerity to honk as the intimidating British mobster strolled across the road as if he were the king of the monsters, stepped right out of a Japanese science-fiction movie. Black was unstoppable, unforgiving, unflappable.

The driver who hammered on his steering wheel to get the annoying jaywalker off the road slumped back down into his seat as Vinnie Black's dark, searing gaze swept across him with the unspoken promise of pain and punishment if they ever saw each other again.

Death was stalking in broad daylight, wearing a suit and coat carved from a black, starless night. He defied the laws of man and nature in his presence, shadow made solid and hard and brutal.

Black stopped on the sidewalk and Sal and Tony fell into step on either side of him, hands crossed in front of their coats to keep their heavy weapons handy and ready for action.

MACK BOLAN WAS ALWAYS ready for action.

As he reached the glass doors of the morgue, he slowed. Three men stood out front, and his instincts read them as London mobsters.

Maybe they were there to avenge the death of Sonny Westerbridge, but the Executioner was doubtful. He had left no survivors who could have seen his features. More likely, these men had been sent by the men he had fought the previous night, and who had gotten away.

The Ripper and his companions.

During their fight, the Ripper would have gotten a good enough look at Bolan's face and body to be able to point him out to his organization. It would be a simple matter of getting people to stake out the likeliest destinations for the soldier.

Heathrow.

The English Channel Tunnel.

The metropolitan police headquarters for Homicide East, where the murder occurred.

The Ripper would know that if Bolan was going to show up and throw another wrench into the works of whatever conspiracy these sadistic killers were hiding, then there was a good chance he'd show within twenty-four hours. All they really had to do was hang back and keep an eye out. If the mystery man who ruined their crime scene disappeared without a trace, then so much the better. If he did start snooping around, then they would be ready to cut him off at the knees. They probably would have felt a sense of impunity at going after him. Even if he did work on the side of the law, they'd have realized Bolan was packing too much firepower to be working for any legitimate law-enforcement purpose in London, especially all by himself.

The Executioner looked over his shoulder at Dean and Goh who were catching up to his long strides, getting ready to follow him through the doors.

There were other people on the steps, but the presence of the three men on the sidewalk had made them steer clear. There was a sense of fear in the air, like the silence in the woods when a hunter stalked through the brush.

The two cops, however, were moving too quickly to pay attention to the threat up ahead, heedless of the trap they were walking into.

The Executioner didn't have to think about what he had

to do. With reflexes born of countless brushes with enemies, he threw himself backward. His body slammed into both of the detectives, knocking them off balance. Simultaneously, his hand dived under his jacket for the tiny Beretta hidden there.

5

Bolan stopped at the glass doors, and Vincent Black saw the flash of recognition play across his face in a millisecond. The big mobster saw the stranger dive into action and he threw himself to the side, knocking Tony into the street. His hand dived for the sawed-off shotgun under his trench coat.

The glass panel of the door turned white, then disintegrated, falling to pieces as Black's shotgun blast and the stranger's handgun bullet went through it at almost the same instant. The mobster heard Bolan's first shot slam into the street behind him, the high velocity 9 mm hollowpoint round gouging into macadam and spewing up chunks of black, shattered asphalt.

Sal stood there for a heartbeat in the wake of Black diving for cover, then reacted, snapping up his shotgun. Thunder burst from the big tube of the 12-gauge, a storm of pellets spraying out in a fireball of destruction that swept the entrance to the morgue.

The Executioner swung back around the entrance. The steel frame of the door shielded him from the storm of Black's second blast as they once more traded fire. Sal stood there, struck stupid. He jerked on the slide of his shotgun and pulled the trigger, hosing the doorway at chest level while Bolan hugged the floor, making the most of the stone steps for cover. Black was certain he could have nailed the warrior if he hadn't had the stone stairs deflecting some of his lower-angled shotgun pellets.

With the cones of devastation blown out by the 12-gauge, Bolan was kept from getting a good angle of fire on his attackers.

Sal jerked hard, spinning. His tan coat went dark over one shoulder, and he dropped to the sidewalk, gasping. Black cursed under his breath, then bit off the urge to turn the sawed-off scattergun against the wheelman when he began howling in pain.

"Vinnie! Vinnie! He got me!"

"Shut up!" Black growled.

Sal looked up at him, his forehead protruding from under his widow's peak and unkempt mop of curls glistening with sweat as his eyes stared wildly. "It hurts so much—"

Black rolled close to Sal, looking for Tony, who was leaning against the front of a parked car, holding his ribs. An automobile with a dent in the hood stood in the middle of the road. The henchman looked pale, and his shotgun was somewhere under the stalled vehicle.

Black cursed. One henchman shot, the other smashed by a car. Already the fight was going tits up, and he wasn't even sure of a single casualty on the enemy's side. Sal clutched at Black's arm, his hands so drenched with blood that he could feel the warm fluid seeping through his coat almost instantly. Black backhanded the man, rolling him into the gutter.

The wheelman's cries were cut short by the shattering of his nose, smashed all over his face. Blood poured down over his lips and chin. With a surge, Black dug under Sal's coat and retrieved the man's Glock with his free hand, stuffing it into his pocket, then going back for the two reloads the jumpy driver always had with him.

"I'm being a little fucking paranoid?" Black growled, keeping an eye on the top of the steps. He punched Sal hard in the face again and rolled away from him. He was tempted to use a shotgun round on Sal, but at that moment, the tall stranger chose to make his assault.

Vincent Black knew when it was time to hold his ground, and when it was time to fall back.

CUTTING AND RUNNING wasn't an option for the Executioner. Not at this point, with three armed killers out front, and an unknown quantity possibly coming around the rear. He could have gambled on it only being the trio out front, but Mack Bolan hadn't survived so long by underestimating his enemy.

Instead, after a quick double-tap that missed, only driving the leader to the ground, he crawled through the wreckage of the front doors, his windbreaker taking most of the discomfort out of dragging himself over the remaining glass in the frames.

"Cooper!" Dean called out.

"Stay back," Bolan ordered.

It was no good. The blond detective was snaking her way toward him. Goh was equally determined to follow on the soldier's heels.

"Do you two have guns?" Bolan asked them.

"No," Dean answered.

"But someone has to at least be in charge of this," Goh added.

The Executioner growled. "I'm not letting either of you get killed."

"We're not looking to get killed," Dean said.

She put her face to the floor as a flurry of shotgun blasts filled the air over her head. Bolan could see that the woman was hating every bit of being the unarmed, helpless victim. She wanted to be in control, and she eyed Bolan's Beretta with envy. He also didn't doubt that the detective could use it.

Every year, the London Metropolitan Police were trained

by their firearms units on the Glock 17 autopistol. While they weren't to carry such weapons on regular duty with them, the police department wasn't so blind as to allow their bobbies to go unprepared for when they were needed to back up their armed-response brethren.

"Stay close to me," Bolan said. He rolled onto his side and extended one leg to Dean and Goh. "Who's the better shot?"

"I am," they both said in unison.

Unfortunately for Goh, he was too far from the .38-caliber Smith & Wesson Centennial in Bolan's ankle holster. Dean plucked the little hatchback-style revolver and did a quick check of the load.

"Five shots," Dean said. "Magnums or Specials?"

"Specials," Bolan answered.

"Shame," Dean lamented. "I'd have liked more punch going against a shotgun."

"I'll take the lead. Cover me," Bolan told her.

"By all rights, you should hand over your other weapon to my fellow officer," Dean said.

"Or you could give me your gun," Goh suggested to Dean. Bolan could see that the Asian cop wanted to risk his own life ahead of his pretty blond partner's.

Bolan ignored them and slithered to the edge of the landing. Dean followed.

The Executioner saw one man standing, fumbling to stuff shells into his weapon. Bolan dropped the hammer on the Beretta, pumping a single 9 mm round into the shotgunner's shoulder and spinning him to the ground. He cried out in pain, but the gangster in black growled at him. From his vantage point, the soldier could see the third of the group, leaning against the front fender of a parked car, nursing a bad injury to his torso.

Bolan realized that he was going to lose his one link with the conspiracy. "That guy in black is going to make a break for it. I need him alive," he said.

Dean glanced at him questioningly. "So…"

The Executioner rocketed to his feet, charging down the stairs. To one side, the injured man leaning on the car was digging in his jacket for his own handgun, his shotgun lost in the confusion that resulted in his injury. Bolan was about to put a bullet into the man when three gunshots melded into one continuous roar.

The gunman was smashed in the arm and chest by a trio of .38-caliber hollowpoint rounds, soft-lead designs that had proved themselves across five decades as the best bullet for their caliber. Bolan knew about them, because that was what he loaded into the revolver he'd handed over to Dean. The mobster's henchman twisted and blood sprayed from his wounds. If he wasn't dead yet, he would be by the time the Executioner's feet hit the sidewalk.

"Call an ambulance!" he heard Dean shout.

Goh gave a loud, unseemly curse, and the sound of hard soles clattered on the stone behind him.

Bolan knew that a chase through downtown London could result in bystanders getting hurt or killed. Fortunately, the mobster was making a beeline for his car. The Executioner didn't pause one step, bringing his little Beretta to eye level and emptying the rest of his magazine into the front tire and fender of the waiting Lexus.

Black scurried sideways as the salvo of bullets hissed past him and tore into his vehicle. He looked back to see the Executioner bearing down on him, a long stick in one hand that he stuffed into the tiny bottom of his pistol. It poked comically out the bottom of his hand, confusing the mobster for a moment before he realized it was some kind of extended magazine. He dived across the hood of his Lexus, tumbling to the sidewalk on the other side just as a fresh pair of 9 mm slugs smacked the windshield in his wake.

The mobster recoiled from the impacts, racking the slide

on his shotgun. As he swung up, he caught sight of the Executioner sliding feetfirst across the hood of the Lexus. Two leather-clad feet rammed Black in the chest and threw him backward, jarring the shotgun from his hands.

Bolan slid off the fender of the Lexus, landing lightly on his feet. He brought up the Beretta in a Weaver stance, the extended 93-R magazine with eighteen shots poking almost ridiculously out of the short butt of the Beretta 9000. Being able to use the larger pistol's magazines was the main reason that the Executioner had picked the little blaster, and he didn't regret the decision.

"Keep your hands up!" Bolan ordered. It took every ounce of discipline to keep from dropping the hammer on Black, but he kept his cool. At the very least, he'd have headaches with the London Metropolitan Police for participating in a gunfight in the middle of a crowded street. Losing his handle on the enemy would be even worse, forcing him to expose himself to future attempts on his life and further battles in public.

His face hardened as he met the mobster's furious gaze.

"You're not gonna shoot me," the craggy Briton said. "I know your type."

Bolan's jaw set, his knuckles whitening.

Black exploded into action, and Bolan's 9 mm round struck the wall just over the hit man's shoulder. The big Briton smashed Bolan across the cheek and nose with his forearm, snapping his head around. Stunned, Bolan let the Beretta fall, but the Executioner was never completely out of a fight.

With all the speed he could muster, he hooked onto Black's forearm and used the fender of the Lexus for leverage, twisting and lifting up the mobster with his knees. The tall man sailed, his long legs kicking in the air as he was vaulted over the car's hood.

Bolan let go of his opponent for a moment and twisted. He shot forward, clawing his fingers under Black's jawline and pulling up hard to ram his head against the sheet-metal hood of the Lexus. A dent formed, and the mobster grunted in pain.

Bolan caught sight of the fist that was aimed at his head and brought his shoulder up to deflect most of the blow. The glancing strike still set his head swimming, but the Executioner pushed down hard on Black's jaw and hammered his fist into the middle of the man's craggy features. Bone cracked and Black's nose folded over. With a defiant roar, the man sat up, pulling free from Bolan's grasp and half dragging him off the car.

"Get down!" Dean shouted.

"Fuck off, bitch!" Black growled, going for his gun.

Bolan heard the Centennial explode twice, and his gut twisted. He scrambled to the street and watched the hit man lurch. He was on the verge of stumbling back into the Executioner. Bolan reached to catch him, to ease him to the ground. Maybe in his last moments, Black would give up the men who put him up for slaughter this day. He'd received such dying confessions before.

"Who are—"

"Sucker!"

Black suddenly sprung to life, seizing Bolan and lifting him up, hurling him toward Dean. Their bodies collided, and they sprawled to the ground in a tangle of arms and legs.

Vincent Black wasn't going to waste time standing still. He could caress and soothe the bruises under his Kevlar armor vest later on, when he was sipping a drink and smoking a cigar. Right now, there was still one more cop on the move, and more on their way.

Kevin Goh pulled out Tony's Glock from where the body had fallen, holding on to the weapon to keep it from falling into the hands of a bystander on the street. But when he saw both Bolan and Dean thrown to the ground like rag dolls, he swung the Glock 17 into action.

"Police! Hands in the air, now!" Goh shouted.

His finger was already tensing on the trigger.

Black didn't pause, going for his own guns—the Glock and the Desert Eagle. Pulling the triggers on both, he sent a salvo of lead spitting at the Asian cop. Goh returned fire, 9 mm slugs slicing across the distance between the two men.

At the width of a city street, both men missed their targets. Firing a pistol in each hand was an up-close and deadly affair, and doing so while on the run made any sort of precision aim impossible. Goh, however, missed his first two shots against the moving target, and had to hold his fire as Black cut behind pedestrians who were cowering beside cars or in front of bystanders huddled in shop doorways.

The detective dived to the ground as Black took another crack at him, having no qualms about hurting innocents. As before, the results were terrible, but when Goh's elbow hit the sidewalk, the confiscated Glock skidded from his stunned fingers.

Black watched the police officer go down, and turned his attention to running like hell when he heard the grunt of exertion behind him. Before he could glance over his shoulder, over two hundred pounds of muscle and sinew slammed into him from behind.

Mack Bolan and Vincent Black crashed into a red-framed telephone booth. It was a testament to the durability of the structure that it didn't topple as nearly five hundred pounds of rampaging muscle collided with it.

Instead, Black twisted hard, hitting Bolan twice in the head with his elbow, anger driving each blow. Only by ducking his head did the soldier deflect most of the fury of the two shots, and he returned the favor, putting two right fists into

Black's back and side. The Kevlar protection dulled the full force of the punches, but it still gave Bolan the freedom of movement to reach up for Black's head. Instinct sent his fingers grabbing for hair, but the buzz cut on the man's head provided nothing.

The Executioner hooked his fingers into Black's collar. Grabbing him by his shirt, jacket and trench coat gave him a thick handle of cloth that allowed Bolan to peel the mobster off the telephone booth. To get more compliance out of the big thug, Bolan kneed Black in the back of his thigh.

Dropped to his knees, the hit man clawed upward, reaching over his shoulders to grab at his adversary's grip on him. Bolan made it difficult for his opponent to breath, twisting his collar until the hit man went red in the face. He eased the pressure, knowing that in this position, it would be too easy to strangle Black to death or to snap his neck.

Black reached back and tried to hook one of the Executioner's legs. With a pivot, Bolan got out of the way in time, but he stepped right into another of Black's punishing elbows, getting hammered right above the hip. The searing pain of a kidney hit unstrung the muscles in the soldier's powerful legs, if only for a few moments.

Black used the opportunity to pull himself around, grabbing Bolan by the arm that still loosely gripped his collar. The Executioner realized that if he held on while the hit man was regaining his leverage, he'd lose the use of that arm for months, even years. A savage kick speared into Black's groin, catching him off guard and folding him over.

Bolan let go. Already he felt the twinge of overextended muscles from Black's sudden reversal. However, he avoided falling victim to an arm bar, which would have snapped the bone in a spiral.

Black wasn't out of fight yet. He still had plenty in his tanks, and he swung up from the ground, catching Bolan just below the navel, knocking the wind out of him, sending a shock wave all along the soldier's abdominal muscles.

Bolan took three big steps back from the kneeling mobster, then stepped back in, snapping down hard into the side of Black's neck. The Executioner's chop was followed by a hard left-handed slap over the hit man's ear.

Black went insensate with pain and rage, clawing his hard fingers into Bolan's belt and forearm, screaming as blood poured from his ear. The Executioner had only meant to stun the big thug, not rupture his eardrum.

It didn't really matter at that point. Any moment now, the mobster would realize that he had guns that he could fall back on, almost literally, and then the sidewalk would turn into a shooting gallery again.

If Black was half-deaf or half-dead for his interrogation, Bolan didn't care. He wanted answers, and he wanted this monster stopped even more. This man was obviously a stone cold killer, and every day he lived, people suffered at his hands.

Bolan kneed Black in the chest, and then raked the joint up into the Briton's chin, bouncing his head backward. Again the Executioner pummeled the craggy killer, knocking the man to the ground.

The brawl continued on. While Bolan had knocked Black back, the British mobster snaked his arm around the Executioner's calf and was holding on tight, pulling him off balance. Both men fell to the concrete, but since the soldier was standing, he had to throw out both hands up to break his fall. His palms were scoured by the hard ground, but he protected himself from a head injury in the tumble. Black took that opportunity to hit Bolan hard in the side of the thigh, a muscle spasm jolting through the soldier from the impact.

Black was blinking away disorientation, trying to keep himself focused. Bolan realized that it wasn't thigh muscle he was aiming for, but to overstress his knee. The Executioner folded his leg, twisting and rolling onto his back. The hit man didn't let go, even though his prey managed to maneuver in his grip.

Instead, Black's hard angular chin was in line for the sole of Bolan's shoe. Bolan launched a solid kick that caught Black on the end of his jaw. The big mobster tumbled, arms flailing, his senses thrown out of order by the nerve-jarring hammer blow.

With his dark eyes blinking slowly, one of Black's hands brushed the butt of his Desert Eagle.

Bolan was still dragging himself to his knees, recovering his breath. He glanced across to evaluate the hulking killer, and saw him going for his gun. Muscles tensed, coiling up like spring steel. With a violent lurch, he was halfway across the space between the two of them when Black's fingers closed around the big gun's butt and swung it toward the soldier's exposed abdomen.

Gunfire ripped through the air. Bolan could feel the force of the muzzle-blast from the .50-caliber slug's exit. White hot gases spilled over him as the 300-grain hollowpoint round sailed just an inch to the right of his rib cage. The power and the fury of the half-inch-thick bullet was expended on the back end of a delivery van, sheet-metal peeling away from the smashing slug's advance.

Vincent Black, on the other hand, screamed as his right leg was destroyed by a trio of 9 mm slugs chopping into it. Melissa Dean held Bolan's Beretta in an aggressive stance, aiming it right at the flattened gunman.

Black twisted to try to shoot at the woman who had dared fire on him, but Bolan landed on him like a ton of bricks, all fists and elbows. After bouncing Black's head off the sidewalk with three punches, he clamped his hand over the Desert Eagle's slide, thumb instinctively sliding the safety lever down. The hammer stood at full extension, and as much as the mobster's forearm bulged with effort, he couldn't pull the trigger and unleash a second .50-caliber slug. Not with Bolan smothering the safety, even when Black tried to disengage the lever himself.

Black hammered a punch into Bolan's ribs, and Bolan returned the favor with a punch to the jaw, all the while, the Executioner's long legs straddling the hit man's barrel-like chest. There was no way that he was going to be driven off this man, not while he was still drawing breath. To let up was to allow a known murderer to run free with one of the most powerful handguns in the world. Already he'd proved a total disregard for innocent bystanders.

Bolan pushed down hard as he felt Black starting to twist his gun free. A punch connected with the soldier where his collarbones came together. The punch could have crushed his windpipe if he hadn't seen the blow coming and straightened enough to pull himself out of reach. As it was, his breastbone hurt like hell.

The soldier squeezed the Desert Eagle tighter, but Black twisted harder. He gained more leverage on Bolan, the muzzle wavering closer to his unprotected ribs.

The Executioner wasn't wearing any body armor.

He weighed his options. If he absorbed the bullet, there was less chance of it hitting someone behind him. His back was facing clear sky. He'd be dead, and unable to continue his war, but Brognola would assign the case to someone else, members of Able Team or Phoenix Force.

The gunshot, so close to his ear, actually made the Executioner flinch, but the spray of brains across the concrete wasn't his own. Ears ringing, stunned by the sudden overpressure of a close range muzzle-blast, he still managed to focus on the profile of his own Beretta 9000, the 20-round magazine sticking out of the bottom of Dean's dainty little fist. His eyes cleared and he looked at her face.

It was a familiar look. The face of your first kill. Her hands didn't shake, and her lips didn't quiver, but her eyes held that wide, disbelieving shock.

She wasn't going to lose it. But this was a jolt to her psyche.

The Executioner glanced down at Vincent Black. There was a small neat hole in his forehead, but the carefully groomed brush of short hair on top of his head was flapping in the breeze, a rooster tail of brains and blood splattering out across the sidewalk like a sideways Mohawk.

Bolan leaned back, looking at the corpse beneath him.

He'd lost his lead on the mystery men coming after him.

And he also learned that they didn't even care if they had to murder him in front of cops.

The killers of the Jane Doe were playing for keeps.

6

This mystery commando is better than I expected, De Simmones thought as he closed his cell phone. Tern watched him out of the corner of his eye, face tight with anticipation of the bad news. And Tern isn't going to let me live one moment down about it. He said he could take care of things, and Black's failure will only be fuel on his fire.

"Your little gangster muffed the job, didn't he?" Tern said.

The words were like a knife slicing into his side. "Is there a reason why you're a right bastard all the time?" was the only response De Simmones could come up with.

"Is there a reason you're wrong all the time?"

De Simmones winced. "You want another shot at him, don't you?"

"I don't see why not. You tried out your second-stringers. Why not send in the top pick and just get this mess over with?" Tern asked.

"What if you get caught?"

"I haven't been caught yet."

De Simmones sneered, then gave Tern a slap where he knew the two .44 Magnum rounds had left painful bruises through the commando's Kevlar. "Nope. Nobody's tagged you yet."

Tern's face screwed up tight, and he dragged De Simmones forward, going face-to-face with him. "Now you listen you old rotting piece of shit. You touch me like that again, and I'll tear your damned head off and shit down your neck."

De Simmones coughed to clear his throat, pulling away. "Who would hire a soldier who couldn't piss because his bladder was blown to hamburger?" he asked.

Tern looked down, seeing the old man's Walther PPK poking him in the groin.

"I might not be able to fight like I used to, but I can make sure that you'll never be useful to anyone else again."

Tern's eyes narrowed.

"This bastard isn't coming anywhere near us, Liam. If he does get close, then you can do something, but I'm making damn sure that no roads lead to me. Got that?" De Simmones asked. "And you are one of those roads leading back to me."

"I didn't know you cared," Tern growled. "Now put that thing away before you blow my dick off."

"I'll keep it out, thank you," De Simmones said, looking out across the hood of the Saab sedan.

"If the ferry guards catch you, there'll be hell to pay. We're not going to kill each other out in public. Get real."

De Simmones considered Tern's words and slid the PPK back into its holster, but he left his hand in his lap, one reflexive heartbeat away from grabbing it if necessary.

"What are we going to do next?" Tern asked.

"Black was killed. But he was the least of my resources there. Well, the least I could summon up and expect some form of success against the kind of man you described."

"No word on whether they found the prime target?"

De Simmones smiled. "No. He'll probably be another day before the smell lets someone know there's a corpse in the room. By then, we'll be long gone, and the toxins will have dissolved from his system."

Tern smirked, looking out the window, watching the waves. "And to think we have them to thank."

De Simmones leaned forward, looking at a bit of white froth in the water, a hundred yards off the starboard bow. "What…oh…"

"Jellyfish."

"I know," De Simmones answered. He took off his glasses and wiped the lenses with the lining of his jacket, hand still poised to go for the Walther. "Actually, we managed to duplicate the venom through recombinant DNA processing. We don't milk—"

Tern locked eyes with De Simmones. "Oh. I was wondering where you put the giant fish tanks and the tiny little poison jugs for those cute little jelly sacks."

"Sarcasm isn't necessary."

"I think it has a certain disarming quality."

De Simmones took a deep breath. "I'm still taking it careful around you."

"You're the one who put a bullet a few inches past my ear and into one of my men because you thought he'd turn into a liability. Ever think that would make someone jumpy?"

"You know I'm a better shot than that. You were taking too much time."

Tern smiled and leaned back. "Well, if that's the case, I apologize for getting up in your gob."

"Apology accepted."

De Simmones sat back too. He didn't loosen his tensed muscles, but he still sat back.

MACK BOLAN TOOK INVENTORY of his latest collection of aches and pains. His muscles hurt, and he sported some new bruises. His ear was still ringing from the close-range gunshot.

"I'm sorry for what I said earlier," Melissa Dean said over the racket in his ears. She came bearing the gift of a can of Coke with a straw.

"Apology accepted," Bolan said, taking the can. He wasn't going to be moving his head around much.

"I could have blown out your eardrum too," Dean told him. "Are you okay?"

"I'm fine. No dizziness."

"I'm not a doctor, but maybe you should have that looked at."

"I should, but I have too much on my plate right now."

Dean folded her arms. "Like what?"

"Jane Doe's murder. And who sent Vincent Black after me."

"It wasn't one of the mobsters who was out to kill Matt Cooper?"

"Why would they be waiting for me at the morgue?" Bolan asked.

"You tell me. You could also help by letting me in on your real name," Dean added.

She was smart, the Executioner gave her that.

"That would be telling," Bolan answered.

She pursed her lips tightly, but her irritation disappeared as quickly as it flared up. "But you were there last night."

It was a statement. Not quite an accusation. But there was no point denying the truth to her.

"I came onto the murder scene and tried to stop the man in the middle of it all."

"And things got worse from there," Dean said, sitting down across from him in at the table. Cops, lawyers, families and others were all around the police station's cafeteria. They all seemed too busy to care about the conversation between the two of them, but Bolan kept his voice low anyway.

"Your Ripper killer, he's as tall as I am, approximately the same build. I didn't see his face. He had his collar up and a cloak that covered most of his features. He had some assistants, but two are injured. One has a bullet through his foot, the other has at least a broken leg from a point-blank ma-chine-pistol burst."

"From a Beretta 93-R," Dean interrupted.

Bolan's eyes narrowed and a smile crossed his lips. "The magazines gave it away."

"Lots of 9 mm brass at the scene. Parabellums and Shorts. Yours must have been the Parabellums."

"Why's that?"

"I don't see you as carrying anything much smaller than a .45."

Bolan nodded. "I'm not sure, but I'd lay even money that the guy with the broken leg is either going to turn up in the river, or won't turn up ever again."

"Why?" Dean asked.

"This was a clean-up. Someone was killing this woman be-cause she either knew something—"

"Or because she did something."

Bolan focused on a small spot on the lid of his Coke can. "Like help in a blackmail. Or a murder?"

"Wait, wait, wait. You're skipping ahead. What about the other two?" Dean asked.

"Like I said. Five men. One Ripper. Two assistants. A driver. And a trained machine gunner."

"Trained machine gunner?" Dean asked.

"He dominated that alley without running out of ammuni-tion. It takes skill to handle a full-powered squad automatic weapon. If it had been just another moron who mashed down the trigger and hosed everything in sight, I would have been done with this and on my way back to America. No, this guy was professional grade. Military training."

Dean looked down at the tabletop. "I can look up records on men like that. Any suggestions of services he'd be from?"

"Royal Marines. Special Air Service. Special Boat Ser-vice. This was a guy who used his weapon to increase the force multiplier of his unit. Even though he was the gunner who had a two hundred round belt in the gun—seven times as much ammo as his partners carried—his job was to make every shot count. A head had to go down, either with a hole in it, or stop shooting long enough for the rest of his unit to get to cover or escape."

"You sound more like a soldier than a cop, Cooper."

"I've fired a few shots in anger."

"And the rest in cold blood?"

"The rest were fired like they were fired today. To protect innocent lives. If it wasn't for the fact that I was trying to take Black alive, the minute he started threatening bystanders, I would have killed him."

Dean's shoulders scrunched tighter against an unseen chill. It was still a fresh experience, to have killed a man.

"Do…" she began. "Do you have anything on the vehicle they were in?"

"It was a black van. Nothing on the plates, and even if I had seen anything, these guys were pros. They went to the trouble to duplicate the original Ripper's style. They would be smart enough to fake license plates or just obscure them with a fine smearing of mud. Once they got about twenty-five miles away from the crime scene, all it would take is a quick splash of water, the plates are clean again, and if they are stopped by the cops, it would be a case of 'Oops. Sorry, Officer, we'll clean off the plate. It must have gotten muddy back so and so.'"

"Picking up mud on a British road? Who'd have thought it?" Dean asked. She got over her initial moment of trauma with a nervous titter.

Somewhere down the line, she'd be alone in the dark and have to face that moment of doubt. Bolan knew it was hard. Even after all his years, there were times when the voice in the dark told him things about himself he almost bought, hook, line and sinker. Only his sense of duty and morality gave him the edge he needed to keep fighting his War Everlasting. Doubt wasn't an option.

"Do you have anything on a possible illegal arms supplier who could have given these guys their weapons? I know that machine pistols are relatively easy to come by…"

"Maybe on an American street, Cooper."

"When criminals need guns, they'll get them. But it takes a special kind of man to get a Minimi-249."

"That's the big gun that produced all that rifle brass in the alley?"

"Yeah."

"Why would they bring that kind of firepower to a simple snuffing of a hooker?" Dean mused.

"Paranoia."

"These aren't American criminals."

"But they are special operations. And being special operations, they're paranoid. They'll pack everything they can fit into a van if they have to, including a backup kitchen sink. Look at me this morning. Sure, you spotted my Beretta. But if you'd have taken that on sight, I still had something up my sleeve. Or more exactly, my pant leg."

Dean eyed him warily. "So they're professionals. They're performing surgical-level hits on women. Nine so far that can be traced to them."

"Clean crime scenes, every one of them."

"Except for the graffiti."

"And that was there to make the whole thing look like a copycat. A calculated effort to distract not only the police, but the press."

"Why the press?" Dean asked.

"Because I think that someone more important might have died. Last night, the day before?"

"I'll check," she answered. "Could be that if they're dead, they haven't been found yet."

"Good possibility. And if they do find a body, chances are that the stiff died in such a subtle way, you'll need Randman to perform an in-depth autopsy. I don't think he'd find anything out of the ordinary, but maybe he'd end up with a non-metabolized trace of whatever killed him."

"Who?" Dean asked. "Who would warrant that kind of killing?"

Bolan frowned. "Lots of people. Politicians. Lawmen. Generals. Reporters. There's enough good people out there that the bad guys are always willing to silence them."

"And you...you're the kind of man who isn't willing to sit back and watch that happen?"

"No."

There was quiet at the table. It was a comfortable curtain of silence, not between them, but surrounding them, cutting them off from the hustle and bustle of the cafeteria. A sense of solace and accompanying relief spread over them both.

Maybe it was because the Executioner didn't feel so alone at the moment. He stiffened again. The pain in his head had left him, but a deeper concern filled Bolan.

The cop sitting across from him had just invited herself into the dark corridors of his world. A place that swallowed the good and the noble without a hint of indigestion.

The Executioner walked alone against the forces of darkness for the simple reason that he wanted to avoid the pain of losing allies. He was a man who tried to keep everyone at arm's length, but sometimes friendships crept in.

Friendships that Bolan had learned all too often led to painful sacrifice.

SHE HAD BEEN SITTING across from a man who had committed one of the largest mass murders in London's history. Melissa Dean could hardly believe she was convincing herself not to do a damn thing about it.

Why should I? she thought. Westerbridge and his mates were nothing but parasites. Murderers who sold death in any form they could market it.

Her hand went to the police identification card in the wallet around her neck. Her face looked up at her from it, and she remembered the oath she'd taken when she was allowed to join the force.

To make places safer. To cut crime and the fear of crime. To uphold the law.

Two out of three ain't bad, she mused. Cooper was a law-breaker, but he did it to take gun-dealing and drug-dealing punks out of circulation. To make places safer. To cut crime and the fear of crime. He just went about it by breaking every conceivable law. Murder. Theft. Obstruction of justice.

She closed her eyes and imagined Vincent Black. His brains were being scrubbed off a sidewalk now that the crime scene was worked over. It was going to be ruled a justifiable shooting, and since Cooper was only acting as an officer of the law in the prevention of violence, he wasn't going to be penalized any more than having the two handguns he'd had with him confiscated.

That's not going to leave a man like him undefended, she knew.

Goh was standing over her when she came out of her introspection.

"How long have you been standing there?" Dean asked.

"A fortnight," he answered. A smile cracked across his face, and he set a foam cup in front of her. "A euro for your thoughts?"

"They're not worth that little," Dean muttered.

"What's wrong?" Goh asked, pulling up a chair and sitting close to her.

"Almost everything. And I'm not sure who to trust."

Goh looked both ways. "You have me."

"Yeah, but would you be willing to look the other way in order to solve a crime?"

"Try me."

"How many thugs would you trade for the life of a single woman? A woman who might even be a prostitute, or a part of a blackmail or murder conspiracy?" Dean asked.

Goh quieted, his smile disappeared. He sat contemplating for a long time.

"Westerbridge reminds me of the triads back when I was on assignment with the Hong Kong Police Department. Big, powerful, bullying. He killed one of our own, and if it had gone to trial, he might even have been able to walk away from it," Goh began. "He had the money, had access to all the right lawyers. Anything we threw at him would have bounced off him like rice."

Dean explored Goh's features.

He continued. "Men like him, they're not afraid of the law of man. So sometimes, you have to go to something higher."

"Kevin…"

"You didn't tell me that Cooper did anything wrong. And Cooper…he wasn't obstructing justice by not reporting the murder last night."

Dean swallowed hard. "I'm sorry to pull you into this, Kevin."

"There's got to be some justice in this world. Westerbridge got his. Who cares who did the job? Nine women are dead now. Maybe more. All because of some conspiracy? That's even worse than if it was a serial killer," Goh answered. "And Cooper has some clues as to what's going on."

"Yeah," Dean answered.

Goh managed a smile again. "What do you need? I'll help."

"Shake a few cages, find out who has a line on big military weapons. Light machine guns in particular. NATO caliber stuff," Dean explained.

"And what will you be looking up while I'm working on all of this?"

"I'm going to talk to my sister. She works at the Ministry of Defense, the Ministerial Correspondence Unit, and I'm hoping that I can get some kind of feel for who would be working for these spooks."

"Cooper thinks the guys are full military?" Goh asked.

"That machine gunner was a professional, according to him. That means he had to be more than just someone who sat on an infantry unit, pumping out half a belt at the first rustle of the bushes."

Goh shook his head. "Vincent Black was the mobster who came after us today. He's a big time leg breaker for local organized crime. Now you're saying we have trained commandos on the case too?"

"Trained commandos. Mobsters. Assassins. A cornucopia of delightful death dealers, all here in our backyard," Dean said.

"What if it's more than our backyard?" Goh asked. "What if this spreads throughout Europe?"

"Killers working for some shadowy movement to undo the mainland? Or just the usual batch of suspects covering up their dirty little secrets? It really doesn't matter," Dean answered. "There's nine dead women, and probably more victims. Innocent people killed because they stood in someone's way. And it doesn't matter why they were killed. I'm not going to sit idly and allow them to murder people."

"I'm going to help you then. I'll follow you through on this," Goh told her.

"Pack light, but pack something," Dean said. "We're not letting these bastards get away with murder."

FOR A MAN WHO HAD BEEN to the ends of the world, it seemed odd that he'd have to come back here. The police station was new, modern and shiny, but built on the remains of the old metropolitan station where he'd been hauled in as a rangy, scruffy teenager, shoved around by police and told that he was a good for nothing troublemaker who would someday earn an appointment with the hangman's noose if he didn't straighten up and fly right.

Well, Rory MacKinnon hadn't learned how to fly, but he knew how to flee a dead-end life. He got himself on the next boat he could and signed up with the French Foreign Legion, knowing that if he was going to be pushed around and belittled, he'd at least get pushed around and belittled to the point where he learned to be the top dog someday.

So when De Simmones called, it annoyed him that he was being yanked off a sedate vacation in Sussex. He was there under the name of David Jones, smoking cigars and drinking brandy and catching up on recreational reading, the kind where you didn't flip the magazine on its side to see the threefold fall open when you reached the middle.

"It's just a simple job," De Simmones had promised.

"Simple means shit, old man," MacKinnon answered.

"Well, I can always give the money to someone else."

"How much money?"

"Thirty thousand."

"Yeah. That's a simple job," MacKinnon repeated himself, doubling his sarcasm.

"I didn't say it would be easy. I've already lost one man to him."

"Anyone I know?"

A moment of silence. "Vincent Black."

"That egotistical fuck couldn't handle a skilled target by handcuffing him to a thousand-kilogram bomb and setting off the trigger."

"Don't speak ill of the dead."

"He got capped?" MacKinnon asked, somewhat surprised.

"Yes."

"And you want me to take out the one who killed him?"

"No. Black and one of his men are dead. But his driver, Sal…"

"I know the bloke."

"Make sure that if he does know anything, he doesn't say it. Try not to make it obvious if you can, and cover your ass."

"I can figure out who to call in on this. They'll be cheap. It'll cost you fifty large, though."

"All right."

"And you expect me to take out the guy who took down Black anyways? He'll be getting in my way."

"Whatever would give you the idea that I'm not being totally honest with you?"

"Your lips are moving, you old fuck."

Not the most diplomatic of bargaining sessions, but the way that De Simmones folded so quickly, nearly doubling the price of the hit, made MacKinnon dead certain that he was getting himself into a rough situation. He had his men, four good tough pikeys who knew their way around shotguns, bare knuckle brawls and knives in the ribs. The English gypsies didn't need much cash to be seduced into doing violent work, and he would pocket the extra cash himself, convincing them that they had ten thousand going in, split five ways.

MacKinnon made sure they had shotguns. He'd have preferred that he was backed up with something sleeker, sexier, more high tech. He reserved a Heckler & Koch MP-5 with a scope, a triple magazine carrier, and a laser sight for himself. It was a beautiful piece of work and if the man was as good as De Simmones said, he'd need every bit of technological edge he could lay his hands on.

Even so, he backed up all of their weapons with a half dozen Browning Hi-Power pistols. The gun was legendary among the British armed forces, and had thirteen rounds of firepower. MacKinnon stuffed two of them into holsters just above each of his kidneys, and he carried two spare magazines for each of the guns in the pockets of his cargo pants. He felt a little foolish carrying that much firepower to snuff out two guys, but then again, Black and two of his mates tried their approach, a simple-enough and quite effective attack of rolling up with three shotguns and continuing to shoot until said target was deceased. When that was done, they'd move along on their way.

Against most people, that was all you needed to do.

Against the target that De Simmones described, it had failed.

Yeah, MacKinnon wished that he could have called in more of his Foreign Legion buddies, and have all of them armed with rifles and grenade launchers.

This would have to be enough, he thought.

After all, this American cop, Matt Cooper, he was just one man. Unarmed and outnumbered, he was doomed.

7

Sal Morris wasn't much of a source of information for Mack Bolan, but when the pickings were slim, you made do with what you had.

The Executioner knew a thing about working with no supplies, poor intelligence and being undermanned. Having Morris to talk to was light-years ahead of some of the situations he had to deal with in the past.

"You're the sot who put the bullet in me," Morris said weakly.

"I hate to sound like we're in a schoolyard, but you started it," Bolan replied.

Morris managed a smile. He wasn't tense, slumped in the bed with his hair matted to his balding skull. "Here to finish the job?"

"I'll let your lawyer get you off if necessary. I just want a few words."

"Would you like 'fuck off' or 'piss off'?"

Bolan shrugged. "It's easy to act tough, but all I have to do is squeeze your nose and lips shut, and you won't breathe again. In fact, with your broken nose, it'd be ridiculously easy to smother you."

"Is that a threat?"

"Just a promise of what will happen if I get disappointed. I don't like hurting unarmed people, and I especially don't like taking advantage of injured men. But in no uncertain terms, you are screwed. I don't care about you as much as I care about the solution to a murder."

Morris looked him over. "So you're doing me a favor?"

"You look like someone who's taken a lot of physical abuse in your life, Morris."

The wheelman straightened. "What's it to you?"

"Why are you suddenly so protective of a man who started beating you up after you got shot? Black is dead."

"So am I if I say anything," Morris replied.

"You might be dead even if you remain quiet. The kind of people who hired Black don't leave dangling clues. If you help me out, I'll help you out."

"Like how?" Morris asked.

"I'll kill the guys who are going to try to shut you up."

"You're a sweetheart."

Bolan smiled. "Do you know who called Black?"

"It's an old guy—named De Simmones. He's not one of Black's regulars. At least he's never called on Black in the whole time that I've worked for him. That's all I've got."

"That might be enough," Bolan told him. "How soon were you guys on my case this morning?"

"You think it was all about you?"

"I know it was."

"Yeah. Vinnie said to follow you. I guess you were getting too close to something. So we were to take you out."

"Didn't work that way."

"Sure as hell feels like it didn't," Morris answered.

Bolan's craggy face furrowed with frustration. "Vinnie wouldn't have a phone book, would he?"

"No. He had a head for numbers. He didn't even trust computers."

"Did he use a cell phone?"

"Of course he did."

"Then he might not have been as thorough with his security as he thought."

Morris looked over Bolan again. "One thing. How are you supposed to provide me with any protection? They took your guns away, didn't they?"

"I'm good at improvisation," the Executioner answered.

The thundering sound of a shotgun rattled through the thin door of the hospital room. Screams could be heard from the hall, inspiring the wounded mobster.

"You better get clever right quick, then."

Bolan grabbed Morris's bedpan and the dinner tray at his bedside.

"Can you move?" Bolan asked him.

Morris sat up, his face whitened, and he slumped back down. "No."

The layout of the room was designed such that when nurses walked in, they would be able to see everything all at once. Bolan set aside his confiscated tools and slid swiftly to Morris's side. Scooping his hands under the man's knees and upper body, he lifted him toward the IV pole set at the side of his bed. Getting him off the bed quickly, he glanced to the door. Doors were being kicked open in rapid succession, from the sound of the racket in the hall.

"What are you doing?" Morris asked.

"Shielding you," Bolan replied. It took all of his strength, and with his battered and tired muscles protesting, he grabbed the hospital bed and turned it onto its side. Pillows and sheets fell away, falling over Morris, who put up his one good hand to protect himself. The bed itself was a sturdy piece of work, with thick steel meant for even the heaviest patients. Hydraulic motors under the metal base panels that folded the bed would provide even more protection against all but the most powerful of rifle bullets.

Bolan's body felt as if it were on fire, but he rushed and

grabbed the bedpan and dinner tray again. The pan was a sturdy piece of metal. The lunch tray was a stiff piece of fiberglass. While they weren't a Desert Eagle and Beretta 93-R, they were better than his bare hands. He stepped just inside the bathroom, far enough out of the view of someone coming in the door to not be seen immediately, but close enough for Bolan to react instantly.

The door was suddenly kicked in, and he heard a heavily accented voice break into a cursed "What the fuck?"

Bolan lurched forward, flipping the tray so that he gripped the edge of it. The Irishman who came through the door looked up just in time to see the Executioner pivot his body and launch the fiberglass platter, spinning it like a discus. The square rebounded hard off the man's face, knocking his head back into the door, the shotgun in his fists held up as if to bar any follow-up attack.

Instead, Bolan went low, following up his attack by swinging the bedpan like a hammer, catching the intruder under the rib cage and knocking the wind out of him. Hot alcohol- and cigarette-drenched breath filled the soldier's nostrils. The Executioner grabbed the shotgun like a handle and twisted, pulling the thug off balance and pulling them both into the hall.

"He's here!" the stunned Irishman shouted, blood pouring from his smashed nose and torn cheek. The guy was as tough as hell, pumping a hard knee into Bolan's ribs and knocking him back against the doorjamb.

Down the hall, Bolan saw four more men. Three of them were armed similarly to the man he was struggling with, but the fourth was carrying a high-tech submachine gun, and Bolan could already see the flare of a laser beam swinging toward him.

"Get him!" someone shouted. It was only luck that put the other three between the Executioner and the gunner. As it was, he dived to the ground, letting go of the heavy shotgun as he did so. Thundering swarms of buckshot sizzled in the air over his head, reminding him how close he was to death. Scrambling on all fours, he reached a laundry cart and swung it around, blocking the hallway and giving himself some room to make an intersection.

"Go! Go! Go!" the leader of this crew shouted.

Luck never seemed to fail. Bolan had needed answers earlier, and had been relatively well armed to face down Black. Now, he had his answer, but he needed firepower.

He grabbed an empty wheelchair and stepped back out into the hall. The gunmen had paused at Morris's room, trying to decide whether to finish off the injured man first, or to chase after their healthy prey. Bolan appealed to their machismo the old-fashioned way.

Flipping them a long middle finger, he shouted, "Come and get it, pikeys!"

"Oh you fuck!" one of the Irishmen snarled, hammering out a 12-gauge blast that chewed out the wall where Bolan's head had been only a few moments before. The soldier folded the wheelchair flat and pressed himself around the corner.

The first man to reach the intersection of hallways caught one of the big wheels of the chair right in his face and chest. He was hammered backward into the two men hot on his heels, their bodies tumbling away in a mass of tangled limbs and snarled curses. The Executioner contemplated grabbing one of the shotguns, but drew himself back behind cover as the dancing laser beam preceded a ripping burst of automatic fire.

Spinning on his heel, Bolan raced down the hall, pursued by the line of fire. With a leaping dive, he skidded across the tile and found the cover of a nurse's station just as Parabellum shockers hammered their way into the countertops. Staff, family and patients screamed as they got out of the way. There weren't too many exits open for Bolan to escape.

Bolan had taken this route because it had the least number of civilian bystanders along it. However, there were still people who could get hurt in the cross fire.

The Executioner was not in the business of getting innocents caught in the middle of his battles. He scanned around. He didn't have a lot of options as far as weaponry went. Nothing that might give him an edge against a gunman with a submachine gun. Instead, he was going to be a sitting duck for the killers once they got their act together and decided to charge the counter he was crouched behind. He saw a doorway, to one side, a medication room that would lead to nowhere and a kitchenette that would turn the corner. He popped up long enough to draw another quick burst from the gunman, then darted for the kitchenette. Just as he suspected, it led to a secondary office, and to a doorway on the far side leading to another hall.

Bolan threw himself forward, swinging the door open wide. He was through just in time to watch a line of 9 mm slugs chop into the door, sending splinters flying. By that point, he was already turning the bend and seeking some kind of advantage.

It came in the form of the man he'd smashed in the face with the dinner tray. Holding his bloodied face with one hand, staggering drunkenly, he didn't notice the mass of pantherlike muscle pouncing on him until it was too late.

With savage quickness, Bolan tackled and rode the gunman to the floor, getting off two quick punches, sending additional explosions of crimson spitting out of torn flesh and crushed cartilage. The man was hard and tough. Even those two punches didn't put him down for the count, and he swung the sawed-off shotgun in his hand like a club. The soldier leaned into the swing, catching the length of the weapon across the thick muscles of his biceps, cushioning the blow. Anywhere else, he'd be contending with a broken joint or a head injury, which would have dropped him so far behind the game that he might as well have rolled over and died.

The Executioner didn't roll over and die for any man.

With a ferocious palm-strike, he drove the jaw of the hired shooter back into his head. Bone crunched as it connected with hard tile and the concrete beneath, and the fighter's eyes rolled up into his head, his body shuddering violently. Bolan spared the man a moment of mercy. Plucking the shotgun from unresisting fingers, he reversed it and pulled the trigger. The fountain of gore and bone chips spread across the width of the hallway, splattering on the walls and onto his jeans and jacket.

There would be time to do the laundry later. Bolan frisked the corpse and found a handgun, a Browning Hi-Power, and a pair of spare magazines.

He stuffed the pistol and the spare magazines into his pockets, and looked up to see the rest of the intruders coming his way.

A plunging dive took him out of the path of their blistering fusillade of buckshot. Tile and plaster flew as the three hired hitters worked their weapons with savage fury. In the chaos, Bolan's shoulder struck a doorway, and the shotgun was peeled from his grasp, the big weapon clattering to the ground.

"He's unarmed!" one of the thugs shouted. Bolan grabbed the Browning from his belt and popped the magazine. There was a full thirteen shots in it, and he thumbed the top round away.

The gun had a reputation for accuracy and excellence, but only because the men who knew how to use it always downloaded the gun by one shot, making sure the magazine wasn't put under too much stress. Bolan slapped the magazine back into place and swung around the doorjamb in time to see one of the Irishmen charging to close range, emboldened by Bolan losing his shotgun.

With almost comic exaggeration, his eyes widened and his boot-shod feet skidded on the tile as he struggled to slow himself. Bolan put him to a complete stop with a bullet that punched through the man's face. As the man toppled backward, life pouring from both sides of his perforated skull, his partners dived into hospital rooms, seeking their own cover.

Bolan pulled himself back, just in time to spot the laser sight's red dot dance across the doorjamb he'd been folded around. Bullets tore into the wall as the Executioner dropped to one knee as the man who seemed to be the leader approached. He was firing short bursts, and Bolan doubted if he'd used even one-half of his first magazine.

The guy edged into the Executioner's line of sight, and Bolan fired on him, burning off two precious shots. The man was quick, ducking away the instant he presented himself. Bolan dived to one side and watched slugs punch through the drywall between him and the hall. Bullets smashed into the empty mattress of a bed and broke the sink and mirror to pieces.

The leader was burning his way through the magazine, but it was in the form of suppression fire. Bolan couldn't move except to retreat, and he wasn't free to return fire with the same frenetic fury because of the possibility of helpless bystanders on the other side of the two walls.

Bolan wasn't even sure if he was packing hardball or hollowpoint rounds, or a mix of both. He glanced back and saw the window to the room stared out into the dark London night. Sliding under the bed, he reached the windowsill and threw it open. There was a foot-wide ledge that gave the Executioner hope that he could draw the enemy into following him. If not, he could swing around the other side and cut them off since the ledge led to an angled rooftop off to the right. He wasn't sure where he'd end up, but anywhere was better than in the middle of a hospital with innocents as potential targets.

He stuffed the Browning into his waistband, crawled out the window and started toward the sloping roof. Near one end, it rose into a steeple where there were four clock faces, and a small bell above it. He figured that if he could reach that, then he could get to ground level and avoid the majority of staff, patients and family who were usually at the hospital. As he reached the end of the ledge, he noticed he had a four-foot leap to the rooftop.

The Irishmen took that moment to burst out the window, their voices booming out curses and challenges to him. One crawled up onto the ledge, almost losing his balance in the mad rush. Only the quick reflexes of his friend kept him from sailing sixty feet to the ground and splattering like an over-ripe melon against the stone floor of the courtyard. That mental image didn't help Bolan's confidence as he turned to make the jump, but he kicked off with all his might, sailing across the empty space, his feet bicycling over the gap beneath his hurtling body.

Bolan landed, both feet hitting the roof's edge. For a moment it seemed like he was unsteadily teetering on the edge, before momentum carried him forward. He turned and dropped onto his back, digging his heels into the roofing tiles as the thugs turned their weapons on him.

A shotgun blast ripped into the shingles to the Executioner's right, and he cut loose with the Browning, tripping off six shots in rapid succession. The first Irishman walked with his back pressed to the wall and took the first trio of slugs along his abdomen. He folded over and as he did so, lost all balance. Hands gripping his ruined guts, he fell headfirst to the ground below.

The last shotgunner worked the slide on his shotgun and caught two of Bolan's shots in his right arm. The bone shattered with one solid hit, and his shotgun toppled to follow the third gunman. With a strangled cry of pain, he tried to pull himself back in reflexive response to being hit, but Bolan followed up and punched a pair of rounds into the shooter's head. He slumped, half in and half out of the window, blood pouring in a torrent from where the Browning's slugs tore massive channels of destruction in his skull.

Four down.

That left the boss man to go. Bolan dropped the magazine from his weapon and fed in a fresh one, stripping the top shot on his reload to insure reliability. Twelve in the magazine, one in the pipe.

The man with the heavy-duty firepower was nowhere to be seen. Bolan glanced to his left, catching sight of the gunman in black slipping onto the ledge adjacent to the roof he was on. Bolan spun, drawing on the killer.

The shooter turned and opened fire too. Both men were moving quickly, and the enemy gunman ducked back into the recessed window. Bolan's Parabellum slugs sparked on brick, while the MP-5 stuttered and kicked up tar paper and roofing nails. The soldier nearly sidestepped off the roof, but caught himself, looking down at the killer he'd dumped five stories below. The dead man's head was a mess of gory blackness against the stark light contrast of the stone floor of the courtyard.

Turning, Bolan raced toward the clock tower, hoping to gain every advantage he could in terms of cover. With five long, vaulting steps, he reached the top of the tower, and slid under the bell just as a firestorm of 9 mm slugs chased after him. The chime resounded, clanging as bullets peppered it.

The Executioner popped up over the low railing and targeted the flashing red lens that was searching for him.

He learned a lesson long ago in the military. Tracers were a good way to see where you were shooting when you were in the dark and had nothing else to see by. But they had one problem—they gave away your position.

Laser sights, the Executioner had learned, and other lighting systems, had the same problem. If you were downrange of one, you'd see the projected beam and know where to aim.

The gang leader was lighting himself up even as he swept to put the dot on Bolan's position.

The Executioner opened fire, the Browning sending its salvo of 9 mm slugs downrange. Here on the rooftop, with nothing but brick and empty space to absorb a stray round, he had no fears of harming an innocent bystander. There was only him and a gunman who'd brought a hardforce into a hospital. And only one of them was coming down easily from this rooftop.

The Irishman lurched hard as he caught one of the Browning's slugs. The Executioner's run for cover had taken him outside of the ideal range of the handgun, especially since he was rushing to get in the first hit ahead of the submachine gun.

It was a nonvital hit, and the gunman tumbled off the ledge. Only at the last minute did he manage to push himself with enough force to land on the rooftop that Bolan had formerly occupied. A parapet rose between the two men, keeping the Executioner from finishing the shooter as he fell into the open.

Instead, Bolan was going to have to get up close and bloody.

Vaulting the railing, the Executioner crossed the rooftop, closing in on his downed opponent, feeding in his last magazine. There was no sign of activity on the other side of the parapet, but that meant nothing. A good soldier knew how to sit still and wait, but Bolan couldn't risk the lives of responding police officers by just hanging back. If the Irishman wasn't dead or dying, he could quite conceivably take down a half dozen of the Armed Response Vehicle force before they put a final lethal round into him.

The encounters with the Ripper and Vincent Black made the Executioner all too aware that these men were professionals, with access to good body armor.

But over it all, Bolan wasn't in the mood for taking any more prisoners.

Not after so many near misses with innocent bystanders.

He looked and saw the MP-5 still on the ledge, across the same four-foot jump that he'd made only moments ago. Bolan looked down at the Browning Hi-Power in his fist, and knew that it wasn't likely that his opponent was completely disarmed. If the shotgunners came with spare handguns and spare magazines, then their leader was going to be packing his own backups.

The Executioner picked up a loose tile and tossed it over the parapet. As it clattered, the barking reports of a pair of pistols filled the air. Bullets sailed into the sky to arc their way over the city.

Bolan shook his head in exhaustion. "Just give up! I have you pinned down!" he called out.

"Not a chance in hell," came the answer.

The man sounded as if he were fast on the road to hell himself. His voice was weakening and raspy, melting away quickly.

Bolan took two steps up, aiming his Browning over the edge. He caught sight of the man for a moment, the right side of his face dripping with a thick sheen of blood. "You're hurt. You're at a hospital. Take advantage of the situation," Bolan said.

The Executioner ducked back as bullets smacked the far side of the parapet.

"Fuck off!"

"You had your chance," Bolan answered.

He lunged and pulled the trigger, punching a line of 9 mm slugs across the black-clad gunman.

As suddenly as it had begun, it was over.

Sightless eyes stared accusingly at the Executioner. He sat on the roof, weary in body and soul from the day's unyielding violence.

As an afterthought, he popped the magazine on his Browning and set it aside. He'd had about fifteen minutes to get a head start on the London Metropolitan Police, and there was no way he was going to test the powers of Hal Brognola's diplomacy by sticking around for the aftermath of two bloody gun battles.

Besides, the Executioner had to find De Simmones.

Judgment day for the conspirators loomed closer.

8

British Army Lieutenant Melanie Dean was staying late, risking inquiry into her activities. But her sister was adamant that she might be able to gather some information on the murderers, men who were formerly part of the country's elite forces, or one of its sister units in Great Britain's special-operations community. The thought was chilling to her, that there could be men who used to be defenders of queen and country that now used their skills to kill for hire.

She wasn't naive, and she knew of the private investigation and security agencies run by SAS veterans across the country. While most of them had the smell of legitimacy, she knew they could be a front for men who were in the business to just make some easy cash, performing violence on a regular basis.

Melanie hated to be reminded that the possibility was there. The hairs on the back of her neck stood up as she worked the search engine for names. One she'd been given was Vincent Black.

According to the records she found, Black was a goon who had lasted exactly six months in the regiment before washing out. The discharge was quick, with little contestation, and that made Melanie curious. She printed out the man's file and went on a search for the next name.

"Simons" was all she had. That, and that he was an old man.

The search took a while, weeding through names like Simmons, Simon and De Simmones. She looked them all over anyway. She deleted men who were under the age of fifty. While there were operators in the SAS who were in their late forties and were known as "the old man" it was usually a begrudged joke on the part of well-liked younger troopers. Anything less usually ended up with a classic tale of how age and guile would whip the tar out of youth and strength. Once an operator hit age fifty, things didn't get so easy, unless the trooper was at the peak of his physical ability.

She narrowed the list down, and one of them was Etienne De Simmones. French spelling and aged sixty-four.

Melanie watched the printout on the screen, looking at his background. The man had large parts of his preretirement history blacked out and classified under "need to know." It was the kind of dossier that made her hands tremble when she held it because she knew the subject was nothing less than death incarnate. Every one of those blackened areas of history was definitely a time where people died.

She knew that those were situations where the dead could have fallen for no more of a reason than the right politician felt someone was blowing the wrong whistle. A dark operation, and suddenly a political scandal disappears in a car crash, or swallows rat poison, or is just stabbed through the chest with a butcher's knife in a desperate mugging.

Or maybe killed by Jack the Ripper, thank you very much, Melanie mused. Melissa had mentioned she was working on a new case in Whitechapel, and it didn't take much in terms of mental mathematics to put together her sister's request and the latest in the line of Jack the Ripper–style murders. Melissa was not the only member of the family capable of deductive leaps.

De Simmones fit the kind of profile that Melissa had stated she was looking for. An old-school veteran, someone with a long and rich history of removing threats to the realm. A memory hit her, and she took up the dossier she had for Black.

Black had been part of De Simmones's squad for the last four of his six months of duty in the SAS. In their service together, both of them were under "blacked out" times.

She heard footsteps coming down the hall and changed her windows, putting a leave-request spreadsheet on top on her computer screen. The friendly, smiling face of Captain Barrie Head poked through the door.

"Staying late after work?" Head asked.

"Unfortunately, Captain," Melanie answered. Head was a nice, charming sort of gentleman, but he seemed to try too hard. There was something about him that just turned her off. "The lads are trying to make sure that their leave is all sorted for the coming year."

"You wouldn't want to put that aside and maybe have a pint down at the Officer's Club with me, would you, Melanie?"

"I would, but then I'd have to disappoint the boys in the morning."

Head shrugged. "I'll wait."

"It'll take about an hour," Melanie said.

"I'm a patient man."

You also can't take a bloody hint, Melanie thought. She glanced at her screen, and knew that Head wouldn't be able to tell what she was working on, but her printouts were going to be a problem.

"Confidentiality. I'll come with you if you wait in the hall, and all that," she said, smiling.

"So you're telling me that I can't know when my men are requesting their leave?" Head asked.

I'm telling you to piss off, Melanie's thoughts burned behind her friendly mask. "I'm just asking for a little privacy because I don't do well while being watched. Give me an hour."

Head smiled. "All right then."

He closed the office door. Melanie opened up the screen and did a name search for all the regimental operators De Simmones was working with. As she hit print, she noticed a flashing icon in the upper-right corner of the screen. She ran her cursor over it.

ACCESS TIMEOUT! FURTHER AUTHORIZATION REQUESTED FROM CENTRAL.

Melanie Dean's heart skipped a beat.

She didn't know who was going to be notified at central, but whoever was being told would eventually come back to her.

Sheets of paper from the list landed in the tray by her right hand.

MELISSA DEAN HEARD the cell phone warble and picked it up on the second ring. The number was her sister's and her instincts kicked into gear.

"What's wrong?" Melissa asked.

"I was doing some checking on those names you wanted. I got the guy you might be looking for, but I may have tipped him off to my interest," Melanie answered.

"Oh hell," Dean grumbled. "Where are you?"

"At the regiment, but I don't think a line of tanks could stop these people," Melanie told her. "Etienne De Simmones is the name I got. He's a longtime vet. Retired from the SAS, but he's been doing work for us. He was linked with Vincent Black, too."

Dean nodded. "Lannie, just hang on. I'll get back to you in a minute."

"What are you going to do?" Melanie asked.

"Call in the cavalry," Dean muttered. She killed the connection and dialed Matt Cooper's telephone number.

BOLAN ANSWERED THE PHONE on the first ring. "Cooper."

"My sister got some information. But she's got the fear of God in her now," Melissa Dean said.

"These people aren't God. They just assume they are," Bolan answered.

Dean wanted to laugh but couldn't. "She's afraid that they'll be sending someone after her. She tripped an access alert. She was looking too long at our boy."

"What name?" Bolan asked.

"Etienne De Simmones."

"I can have my own sources look into him," Bolan said. "She's where?"

"Whitehall. The Old War Office Building just to the south of Pall Mall," Dean answered. "I was hoping you could get there before De Simmones sends someone to kill my sister."

"I'm pedal to the metal here. Are you going to meet me there?"

"I'll do my best," Dean said. She nodded to Kevin Goh, who was getting behind the wheel of his Jaguar XK8. "You also won't have to worry about supplying the party favors this time out."

"Guns and speeding, a wonderful combination," Bolan said.

"Ask him if he's interested in the fact that someone tried to kill Sal Morris," Goh said. "Tell him that fortunately, some stranger saved Sal and a whole lot of innocent bystanders."

"I don't think he needs to be worried by such trivia," Dean answered.

"What trivia?" Bolan asked.

Dean smiled weakly, if only to make herself feel better. "There was some drama at the hospital where Sal Morris was recuperating."

"Nope. Not interested in such trivia," Bolan answered.

"Thought not," Dean stated. "Kevin, hit it. Cooper, what are you going to do in case you get pulled over?"

"I don't intend to. Besides, my license plates are too muddy and I drive too good for the police to catch me."

"I'll pretend I didn't hear that," Dean answered. "No. I did hear that. How fast can you reach her?"

There was a pause.

"Call your sister. I'll be there in twenty minutes," Bolan said. "Tell her to get out in the open. I'd recommend Westminster Bridge. I'll pick her up there."

"And what if they get there before you do?" Dean asked.

"Asking those kinds of questions only takes time away from the accelerator."

THE REAR WHEELS of the BMW Z4 slipped for only a second as the Executioner kicked the silver sports car into gear and took off down the road. Twenty minutes was a highly optimistic estimate of how fast he could make it from the Royal London Hospital south to the Tower Bridge, through Lambeth and to Westminster Bridge. With a powerhouse machine like the BMW, barring any incident with the local police or an accident, he could make it. Traffic would be the killer here.

The Executioner was willing to risk his own life to save a life. Bystanders, however, were always a concern. They'd been dogging him all day, and now, he was trying to get through the relatively light nighttime traffic of one of the largest, busiest cities in the world.

Only once did a police car try to clue in on his tail after he pulled away from the Tower Bridge and onto St. Thomas Street. Bolan's mastery behind the wheel simply left them in a mud spray, the silvered skin of his land rocket splattered along the sides and back with a smear of browns and grays he'd deliberately hosed across the formerly gleaming machine. There was no good description of his car as he sped along. That much he was aware of from working the multi-band radio scanner in his war bag. Having his ear on the pulse of the local police was a boon to him.

Like the night before, when he listened in on the voices of Sonny Westerbridge's men, knowing what the enemy was thinking about and talking about was the first step in forming a plan. He cut north to avoid potential roadblocks, and as soon as he reached St. Thomas's Hospital—right off of the Westminster Bridge—he powered west again, making up for lost time by red-lining the BMW up to 160 miles per hour.

It was a testament to both the Executioner's skill and the car's engineers that he stuck to the rain-slicked streets, avoiding slower-moving cars and bypassing pedestrians without harm. Bolan didn't like flagrantly breaking motor safety laws, especially not behind the wheel of a ton and a half of high-performance vehicle.

But someone was counting on him. Bolan was halfway across the bridge when things turned. He stood on the brakes, bringing the Z4 to a halt, running it up onto the walkway of the bridge. A truck had overturned in the middle of the bridge, blocking several lanes, more traffic clogged either direction, trying to cut through.

Bolan didn't waste time cursing his luck. Instead, he pulled out his cell phone, grabbed his war bag and ditched the BMW. Melanie Dean's number was a quick tapping of his thumb on the keypad.

"Hello?" came a nervous response from the other end.

"My name's Matt Cooper. Your sister told you to expect me," Bolan said quickly. "Are you armed?"

"No."

"Are you in public view?"

A pause on the other end. "I'm waiting at the mouth of the Underground station at the end of the bridge."

Bolan could see that squeezing past the crumpled nose of

the truck was going to be tough as it pressed hard against the railing on the bridge. A couple of traffic control officers were waving back cars and trying to control the gridlock on the other end.

One was walking toward him with a purpose, having noticed the ditching of the sports car.

"Melanie, you're going to have to stay in the open, but don't expose yourself to any tall buildings on the land side of the station," Bolan said. "Keep your back to a wall and watch the roads along the water. I'll get right back in touch with you."

"Here now," the cop began as Bolan hung up.

"One second," Bolan said. He was already speed-dialing Detectives Dean and Goh. Dean answered after one ring. "Don't take the Westminster Bridge. She's at the Underground. Hurry!" he said.

"We're on the other side of Lambeth yet," Dean answered.

"Could I have your attention?" the lawman before Bolan asked.

"Sure," the Executioner said, flipping the phone closed. He pocketed it and slung the war bag across his back.

Bolan slugged the policeman hard in the jaw. It was a textbook perfect knockout punch, and he caught the man before his legs turned to useless rubber beneath him. Lowering him gently, he called out.

The cop's partners looked on in confusion wondering what was going on. Two ran to him while the others continued their traffic control work.

"He just fell down," Bolan said to them. They appeared to be buying it, as their concern was more with the dazed lawman than with him.

With a burst of speed, Bolan took off. When he reached the crashed truck, he grabbed hold of the hood for support, climbed up onto the railing and slid across it, coming down on the walkway on the other side of the blocked bridge. There, another lawman watched in surprise as the big American landed.

Bolan gave the man a salute and jogged along, heading toward the opposite end of the bridge. It took a few seconds for the oddity to register, and the cop shouted after the Executioner, footsteps signaling the beginning of a chase.

All of this was delay. Bolan let the policeman catch up with him, then pivoted into the man, catching him with his elbow across the cop's sternum, sweeping his foot into his ankles from behind. The traffic cop tumbled dazedly to the ground.

Bolan cut into the line of cars, snaking and weaving among them, losing himself in the gridlock while the policemen behind him dealt with other problems.

MELANIE DEAN LOOKED around her as she backed against the street-level entrance to the Underground. With the shell of the entrance between her and most of the buildings inland, she felt relatively secure. No buildings less than a mile away were in position to give a sniper a good shot.

Not that she would know what a good sniper's hide would be with a manual and a telescope. She chewed her lower lip and thought about what she could do. Any kind of movement would be tantamount to suicide, but if she stayed put, she felt even more exposed to potential violence. She looked at the sheet of printouts in her hand and realized that, if anything, her sister needed to get the papers.

Cooper had asked if she was armed.

Fat chance of that. But she wasn't going to die like a helpless sheep. Under the pretense of stooping to adjust her shoe, she slipped the wad of papers uncomfortably under her heel.

Provided Cooper showed up in time, she'd kick off the shoe and hand him the paperwork. Already she could feel the uncomfortable lump stretching the tendons in her calf and the arch of her foot.

Her phone rang.

"Melanie?" Cooper's voice came through, clear and strong over the cell.

"I'm here. Where are you?"

"A truck crashed on the bridge. I'm on my way though," Bolan promised. "So's Melissa and her partner."

Melanie rose to her full height and spotted a tall man, in uniform, walking toward her. There was something familiar about him, but he crossed her vision on the other side of a swarm of people just getting out of the Underground station. Her heart jumped for a moment.

"I saw someone. I think I saw someone. I'm not sure," Melanie answered. "You have the name, right?"

"Etienne De Simmones. Yeah. But I'm coming," Bolan said. She could hear him running on the other end. Glancing up, she saw a man running toward her, cell phone to his ear in one hand, a heavy satchel in the other. He was trying to cross the street to get to her, but traffic was too thick.

Melanie looked around and saw the man who'd frightened her. He ducked out of sight around the corner of the station's entrance. She looked down at her feet, then slipped her foot out of the shoe.

"Cooper…catch," she said. She could feel the presence of her stalker swinging around behind her, but she scooped up the shoe, hauled back and threw it with all her might.

That's when she felt the one-two punch of a pair of silenced bullets strike her in the rib cage. She looked around accusingly and saw the face of Barrie Head looking down on her. She remembered seeing his name on the list she printed up.

Darkness swirled around her, and she coughed something

thick and coppery into her mouth. Breathing became so hard, and then her knees gave out just as she heard the sound of screams.

As soon as Bolan heard Melanie call for him to catch something, his eyes were split between a woman throwing something toward him, and a man lurching out of a hiding spot, triggering a gun, the sound-suppressed weapon's muzzle-flashes something only his experienced eye would pick up.

Dread filled the Executioner's gut as he swung his arm through the handles of the war bag and reached up, grabbing the well-thrown shoe. A wad of crumpled papers was stuffed into the toe, and the dread deepened. Melanie Dean had given her life for a cause he'd employed her in, no matter how peripherally.

Another one of Bolan's friendly dead, and the lean man with the half-moon profile who killed her was turning into the Underground station to get away.

Traffic be damned, Bolan charged across the street. Cars stopped, horns blaring as he wove between them. With his other hand, he was already calling Melissa Dean.

He'd sooner have faced the murderous sniper at this moment, but he needed her to know about what happened, and the danger she would be heading into. If there was any luck on Bolan's side tonight, he would be after the man who killed her.

And if there wasn't any luck, then God help Etienne De Simmones and all the armies he could muster.

There wasn't going to be an ounce of mercy left in Mack Bolan's heart for any man aligned with the Rippers.

Melissa Dean dropped the cell phone as Kevin Goh brought the car around, tearing up the road south. She hadn't known that this day could get any worse. Now, horror plowed through her like a spreading infection, an infestation that sparked from the center of her being and out to the tips of her fingers and toes. Blood rushed in her ears as she tried to maintain her balance while Goh navigated the Jaguar.

"What's wrong?" Kevin asked. His voice sounded distant and muffled. She wondered if it was the aftereffects of all those gunshots earlier that day, or maybe she'd been going too long without sleep and her brain wasn't working anymore....

"Melissa?" Goh asked again, trying to keep his eye on the road and look after the stunned woman as well.

Dean felt like her tongue was an inert lump of deli meat, stuck in her mouth. "Melanie...she's been shot."

"Christ," Goh answered, his face going white.

Almost automatically, she reached for the handgun in her purse. She'd gotten the little blaster off a Project Talon task force member who knew that there were times when even an ordinary police detective would need access to a high quality side arm.

"Melissa, are you okay?" Goh asked. He sounded nervous. She glanced down at her hands and realized that she'd pulled the Kahr K40 out and was brandishing it in the front seat. She didn't worry. The gun had a safe double-action trigger pull.

"Get me there, Kevin...please..."

He nodded. "Anything."

THE KILLER DIDN'T HAVE much of a lead as the Executioner cut down the stairs after him. Bolan tried to take this one by the book, to give Melissa Dean a chance to deal with this scumbag in the right manner. He called out after the man in uniform. His sense of duty to Dean kept him from simply dialing in the front sight on the Desert Eagle and launching a .44 Magnum slug through his skull.

"Stop! Police!" Bolan challenged.

Captain Barrie Head paused, then looked up the stairs. His face loosened, long lean features turning and swimming in a torrent of emotions. Some part of him was probably wondering if surrender was an option. Unfortunately, the part controlling Head's gun hand was swinging the suppressed Glock up, aiming it at Bolan's heart.

Bolan twisted to one side, throwing himself over the brass handrails separating the wide staircase. At the same time, he let centrifugal force snap the handles of his war bag into his hand. Head's first shot struck the heavily padded nylon and Kevlar satchel, stopping cold. Bolan hurled his well-wrapped wear bag at the renegade soldier as an improvised missile, catching the man full in the chest and knocking him down the rest of the stairs. People screamed and got out of the Executioner's way as he charged down after Head.

The British soldier got up, moving slowly, hand slapping the marble floor for the Glock pistol he'd dropped. Bolan was nine steps from Head and knew that he wouldn't be able to make it in time to stop the killer from grabbing his gun. Everything told Bolan that he should slap leather and pull out the Desert Eagle, slicing the guy in two with a salvo of 240-grain hollowpoints, but instead, he leaped, long legs propelling him across empty space.

He came down on Head's back, knees crashing between the guy's shoulder blades. Folding and tucking in, Bolan landed on his shoulder and rolled across his back, feeling the marble floor grind the crosspiece of his shoulder holster deep into the flesh of his back.

Bolan rolled to his feet, seeing Head flattened on the ground. Blood poured from his nose, and his chin was raw and livid where his face had crashed into unyielding stone. Bolan grabbed him by one wrist and twisted his arm around his back.

"Not very tough against someone expecting you to shoot

him, are you?" he growled, grabbing Head's other wrist.
From his back pocket, he pulled a nylon cable tie and
wrapped it around both wrists.

"Get off of him," came an angry voice from up the steps.

Bolan didn't recognize the voice at first, but he turned to
see Melissa Dean, her face a mask of shattering sanity holding back a flood of rage.

He also noticed the unwavering .40-caliber muzzle aimed
directly at his head.

9

With his hands full restraining the murderer, with the gun aimed at him, and with the familiar look of a spiritually shattered Melissa Dean on the verge of coming apart and taking a chunk of the world with her, Mack Bolan stayed very still. Only his arms flexed, applying tendon-stretching and muscle-ripping force to Head's limbs, making him cry out in discomfort as he ground harder into the tile floor.

"Ease the hell up!" Head growled.

"Be quiet," Dean answered. She punctuated her response with a single shot that chewed a divot of white tile inches from Head's skull. The downed renegade gagged.

"Don't let her…" Head began to blubber.

"Why shouldn't I? You murdered her sister," Bolan stated.

The gun swiveled back toward him, and he regretted that reminder.

"He wasn't the only one," Dean said. She took another few strides forward, descending the steps, the gun locked on to Bolan's face as if there were an invisible magnet connecting them. Bolan knew that she was a good shot, and abstractly, he found himself unable to fault her form.

Another part of him wanted to howl in sorrow. He knew the feeling of loss that surged over her right now—a choking, strangling thing that had broken men who had fought off hordes of enemy soldiers without batting an eye.

That crushed spirit, that impotent anger, of not being able to ever tell your sister you loved her again, that you'd never see her across the table, share a joke, listen to the latest news and gossip about her life…

He tried to reach out to her. "Melissa…"

"He shot her. But you…"

"I was stopped."

Dean's mouth turned up at the corner, a half smile that didn't reach the rest of her face. Instead, her knuckles only tightened around the grip of the Kahr. "You let her down."

"I'm sorry. If you're going to do it, do it," Bolan said calmly.

Dean moved closer, but stayed longer than an arm's length away from Bolan. She wasn't going to be disarmed. Again, he mentally complimented her on her excellence of form. She would have made an top-flight American cop on a high-risk arrest team.

"Do what?" Dean growled.

"Pull the trigger. Pull it if you want. You nearly blew his brains out."

"Melissa!" Goh shouted from halfway up the steps. They were cleared now, the crowd milling at the top, the station platform itself filled with only a few people who'd pressed themselves flat to the walls.

They knew what to do, Bolan thought. The Tube, despite the London Metropolitan Police's reputation for keeping crime down, was still a violent place. This was just unusual in that there was the threat of gunplay.

"Why did you let her down?" Melissa asked.

"Melissa, they're calling in an AVR," Goh told her. "Put the gun away before there's trouble."

"My sister's dead. That's plenty enough trouble!" Dean snapped back.

"You're the only person alive who ever had her sister murdered?" Bolan asked.

"Oh, you empathize?" Dean asked.

"I've been there. I took out that anger on a lot of people who I felt were responsible for her dying, my mother dying, my father blowing the top of his own head off," Bolan whispered. "You want to act like you own the market on suffering? Fine. But pull the trigger on me or put that gun away. I'm not afraid of being shot. I'm not afraid of dying. And I'm not afraid of owning up to my responsibilities and failures."

Dean didn't waver. She put the Kahr away smoothly and carefully. She glowered at him. "We're not fucking done with this."

Goh, on the stairs above her, stuffed his pistol back into the waistband of his jeans.

Two SO14 officers appeared at the top of the steps, one armed with a Glock 17, one armed with a Heckler & Koch rifle. Bolan held on to the murderer.

"Police! Freeze!" the two officers challenged.

Goh held up his badge. "Homicide East! Apprehending a suspect."

"Keep your hands up!" the officer with the rifle ordered. The black rifle was aimed right at the center of the Asian cop's chest. Bolan knew that the weapon was highly accurate, capable of hitting a melon-sized target at three hundred meters with its built-in scope. If Goh made the wrong move, he would be chopped in two and not even feel it.

The second one, the one armed with only a handgun, approached Bolan and Dean. "You two..."

Dean stepped back to the wall. Bolan could feel the burning rage, the smoldering scent of impotence wafting off her. Her face was a mask, a mask too hard, almost too brittle to hold up for long, but he hoped that she could hang in there.

Bolan stood up, backing away from the downed man. He nodded toward the pistol kicked near the edge of the platform. "There's the perpetrator's pistol, Officer."

"Who the hell are you?" the cop with the Glock asked. He was in good form too. Bolan didn't know the statistics on London policemen shot with their own side arms, but from what he'd seen today, he figured they were marginal at best.

"Detective Matt Cooper," Dean spoke up. She showed her badge, and her voice was under control, the words coming out clipped and quick. "He's working on the Ripper case with us."

The SO14 officer gave Bolan the hairy eyeball, then lowered his gun. He didn't put it away, he just aimed the muzzle at the ground, ready to come up. At all times, the policeman kept as much of his blue Kevlar vest between them as possible. He held out his hand for Dean's badge.

She dropped it right in his palm, all business.

"That's legit," the policeman said. "I suppose you're clear too, despite the hardware you were packing."

"We were coming to a situation where a high-risk arrest might have gone down," Bolan answered. "I like to travel well-equipped."

"And the woman upstairs?" the officer asked.

"She was doing some investigating for us," Dean answered. "She's…she was…her name is Melanie Dean."

The SO14 officer's eyes met hers for a moment. There was a little glimmer of her trauma released in her voice, and he nodded. "I'm sorry. Is this the…"

"I was just going to start asking him questions," Bolan answered, slipping into the persona of a tough Boston cop in vengeance mode.

"We don't do that Torquemada routine on this side of the pond, Yank," the officer said. "Get off him. Hopefully you didn't break as many of his bones as you broke of his rights."

Bolan shrugged. "One can only hope."

He locked gazes with Dean.

She wasn't glaring at him anymore. She was staring through him, in a world all her own.

MACK BOLAN OPENED his eyes and sat up, shrugging against the cold that stuck to him past the gate of dreams. Melissa Dean was standing over him, holding a cup.

"How long was I out?" he asked.

"An hour. I figured you needed the rest," she answered, sitting across from him.

Bolan took a sip. It was a sweet, extremely strong coffee. His eyes blinked awake almost instantly. He remembered being given the opportunity to rest in the break room at Homicide South's offices while the Metropolitan Police checked out their reasons for being out of their normal jurisdiction without consulting the locals.

From the look on Kevin Goh's face, the hostility that would have been in place in a U.S. jurisdictional conflict wasn't happening. Things were going smoothly.

"How much?" Dean asked.

Bolan switched to looking at her. "How much what?"

"How much does it hurt? This can't be all of it," she mentioned. "I'm still able to walk, I'm still able to talk. I can think…when does it all hit you?"

"I can't answer that. But I do know—when it first happened—there were times when I was absolutely paralyzed with pain."

"What did you do?"

"I focused on making sure nobody ever hurt like I did again."

Dean looked at the floor. "That didn't work out."

Bolan sipped the coffee. He wanted was the caffeine coursing through his blood and kicking him back into action.

"I'm sorry, Melissa."

"I'll live," Dean responded. "If not, I'm taking some bastards with me."

"Don't talk like that," Goh spoke up. "We're going to solve this, and we're going to walk away from it in one piece."

"That's my goal," Bolan told him. "I have enough guilt on my hands with old friends and partners dying. I don't need a new one."

"Enough morbid thought," Goh stated. "I have news from Dr. Randman. Two big chunks of important news. The X-ray problems were due to radioactive residue left in the woman's body—"

Bolan interrupted. "They couldn't get a good image, that meant overexposed film. Overexposed film means some form of radioactive residue. And that's how they tracked this woman."

Goh was stunned. "Tracked her?"

"She had a small scar where something was inserted into her," Dean said. "But radioactive…"

"Low yield. We're not talking an ingot of weapons-grade plutonium. More like a pellet of stuff that shouldn't be more radioactive than the night-sights on your average SWAT pistol," Bolan explained. "But even that much is enough to be picked up by sensitive equipment."

"Why would they need to track her?" Dean asked. "This is confusing. All of this, the SAS-trained killers, women butchered, all for what?"

"A newspaper editor was found dead in a hotel about two blocks from where the woman was found in the alley," Goh stated.

"A newspaper editor?" Dean asked.

"*The Clarion Cry*," Goh added.

"That's a radical newspaper. They're always exposing some kind of government conspiracy, whether it's kickbacks for farms underproducing food, or it's the transcript from Princess Diana's final audio journals," Dean explained to Bolan.

"Randman didn't find anything physically wrong with him, but the tests showed that the time of death was slightly before the end of our girl, give or take an hour," Goh continued.

"That doesn't mean anything. There are neurotoxins that are totally untraceable without proper testing," Bolan pointed out.

Dean mused out loud. "So our girl killed this editor with an untraceable poison..."

"Probably in a way that the woman who performed the kill wouldn't even know herself, especially if she was hopped up on enough heroin," Bolan surmised.

"That's pretty complicated. Why not just put a bullet in someone's head? Why neurotoxins and a trained commando impersonating Jack the Ripper?" Goh asked.

"The Ripper murders are all across the newspaper headlines. Even *The Clarion Cry* is riding this story," Bolan said. "We find a small radical newspaper's editor is dead, and that won't even dent the mainstream newspapers. Meanwhile, *The Clarion,* if it does hint at foul play, will just be brushed off as more conspiracy theory lunacy."

"Paranoids are always crying wolf," Dean spoke up.

"Any idea what story he was working on?" Bolan asked.

"Triads," Goh said. Then, "You're not paranoid if they really are out to kill you," he muttered.

"Speaking of which," Bolan said. He leaned over and checked his weapons in their bag. Nothing had been disturbed. "What are you two packing?"

"I've got a Smith & Wesson Centennial," Goh said.

"The Kahr .40 you saw before," Dean added.

"Either of you okay with Beretta pistols?" Bolan asked.

"Yeah," Goh answered with enthusiasm.

Dean nodded. "The little lever on the top lowers the hammer. A forward thumb stab pushes the safety back off. It's pretty fast. Not as fast as a Glock, unless you carry it with the safety off," she said.

"Which is possible. They do have the double-action triggers and firing pin safeties," Bolan told her.

Dean took one of Bolan's spare Beretta 92 rigs while Goh got a second. He normally didn't share his arsenal, but he knew that the two cops would come under as much scrutiny as he would. Anything they encountered would need a lot of firepower to solve.

Dean took a few turns at flicking off the safety, getting a feel for it on the draw. The forward sweep of her thumb struck the spring-loaded lever and clicked it readily. Satisfied she could operate the gun under duress, she loaded the magazine back in, racked the slide to get a round into the chamber, dumped the mag and topped it off before putting it back in the handle of the pistol.

Professional handling all around.

Goh was equally adept with his Beretta, although he was a little more cocky with the way he held his gun, one eye squinting at the handsome lines of the big 9 mm. He grinned, flicked on the safety, and stuffed it into the holster, tucking the gun into his waistband. "Ah… that's a pretty thing."

"We have a plan for after we're done here?" Dean asked, sounding a little impatient. Bolan understood that. He wanted to get back to work too.

"De Simmones. We look him up," Bolan stated.

"How? He's probably gone into hiding by now," Dean said in exasperation.

"Not really. Cooper's been making no bones about his investigation. I think you've been doing that on purpose," Goh said.

Bolan shrugged. "It usually works to have your enemy come after you. I just hate that they've been coming after me in crowded places."

"So why not lead them into a trap?" Dean asked.

"I've been looking to try that. But waiting for my enemy

to come to me is grating. I've been too passive so far," Bolan said.

Goh was incredulous. "You call six dead men in the course of one investigation 'passive'?"

"I call it a slow start. But don't worry. Things are going to pick up now," Bolan promised. He held up the list of names that Melanie Dean gave her life to acquire. "Where they fall, I don't care. As long as they point me toward De Simmones."

ETIENNE DE SIMMONES PUT the phone down, knowing full well that he was under the baleful glare of Liam Tern, a gaze that bored through him, reading the news of failure off his body language.

"How many lost now?" Tern asked.

"Head. MacKinnon. A bunch of his crew."

It was a laundry list of their connections back in London, a toll of half their resources for information, manpower and matériel. De Simmones took off his glasses and squeezed the bridge of his nose, knowing that this wasn't going to be an easy road.

"I told you, I told you and you didn't believe me."

"We're in another country, Liam."

"Don't give me that, old man," Tern growled. "This guy, I know his type. We don't try to kill him twice, and then leave him be. He'll hunt us down. He'll come clawing after us. Hell, he killed Head, our man down at the ministry."

De Simmones tensed, knowing is next statement would spark an explosion. "He didn't kill Head. He's in jail. He's in jail because he killed some bitch who tripped the alarms I put on my records."

Instead of an eruption of fury, he looked up and saw Tern standing there, his face split with a wide grin. De Simmones always wondered why the man volunteered so readily to duplicate the crimes of England's most notorious serial killer.

The rictus etched across Tern's face now told the whole story—a tale of repressed fury and madness. De Simmones remembered he had picked the man because he was one who would be untroubled by a little, or a lot, of blood spilled here and there.

He never realized that deep inside, Tern was just as cold, or even colder than the original Ripper might have been. On a metaphysical level, De Simmones was fascinated by this transformation before him, from angry soldier to gleeful murderer. On a practical level, he was glad for the Walther in its hiding spot.

"Etienne, there's no reason for us to be going back and forth, accusing each other of incompetence."

De Simmones bristled at the sound of his first name. "I don't know who the hell you think you are, but—"

"I'm the one in charge now, Etienne," Tern said softly. "We'll handle this mystery man my way. And if I have to, I'll deal with you if you cause me too much trouble."

"The people who hire us…who pay our bills, they're not going to like working for someone who has multiple personalities."

"There never was a multiple personality," Tern said, stepping closer. "Just an act. An act I put on for the world. God, the queen gave me a rifle and a bayonet and taught me how to kill. And then she said I could only do that in times of war."

De Simmones took a step back, his heart hammering.

"You were the one who gave me my next big break. The gay reporter who was writing that article about the radiation leak from one of our pocket nukes in Germany. The housewife who stepped out onto the back porch as we were sneaking up on those Palestinians in Paris. Bigger, more satisfying steps."

"And the temper?" De Simmones asked. "Where did that disappear to?"

"I'm still mad, but I've got it under control…for now. I'm saving it, saving it for that big bad man in black I fought with. The man who stepped in on my playtime with the lovely young lady."

"You've gone strange."

Tern shrugged, his knife suddenly glimmering in De Simmones's peripheral vision. "They say that the first step to redemption for a lunatic is to know that he's mad."

The edge scraped along De Simmones's cheek, before Tern slid the deadly blade back into its forearm sheath. "Why do you think I play Bloody Jack, my friend? Because I know I'm the bedrock of sanity?"

Tern stepped away, and the old soldier put his hand on his gun. A cold, hard glare froze De Simmones like the freeze frame of a photograph.

"You can try to kill me, and then I will tear your kidney out, and just for shits and giggles, I'll mail it to Scotland Yard. From Hell and all that rot."

De Simmones let his hands fall to his sides.

He'd just surrendered control of everything, including his life, over to Tern.

10

It was time to stop playing the game by the enemy's rules and to start doing things his way. Mack Bolan had never been the type of man to sit back and allow the savages to assault him.

Bolan was the supreme predator in a forest full of scavengers.

With a handful of information, he could track down, shatter a network of thugs, and leave their plans in broken disarray with a day's effort, even less if he was truly on a rampage.

It was rampage mode. The Ripper and De Simmones were going to feel every ounce of his persecution.

The plan was simple, one the Executioner had used countless times before. Lean on the enemy. Lean on the enemy's friends. Lean on the enemy's enemies. Apply as much pressure as possible until his target popped into view.

Then drop the hammer.

It's what Bolan had done to Sonny Westerbridge only a few days before.

Back in the old days, cops watching him pull apart Mafia Families had dubbed this the Bolan Effect.

Bolan preferred to think of it as letting the bad guys reap what they've sown.

THE CAR ROLLED TOWARD the metropolitan police station where Homicide South was holding Barrie Head. The sedan looked official enough, colored in a nice army green with flags and stickers across the sides and on the corners proclaiming its use as a British army official vehicle. Inside were three men: the driver, a man in a sergeant's uniform riding shotgun and a man in an army captain's uniform in the back seat.

They traveled in brittle silence until the driver paused the sedan in front of the police station, letting the other two occupants of the vehicle out.

There was some dispute over whether Barrie Head was going to be held by the British army for murdering a fellow officer, or by the London Metropolitan Police. While phone calls were being bandied between both sides, the rank officer walked to the front of the station. The man in the captain's uniform was being kept updated on the proceedings between the two jurisdictional offices thanks to the little cellular phone he was holding to his ear. He reached the door to the station.

He stopped cold.

Six foot, three inches of icy-eyed fury blocked his entry.

"You can turn around and tell De Simmones that he's no longer in charge, or I'll just pin the note to your corpse," Mack Bolan informed the man dressed as a British army captain.

"You son of a bitch…how?" The man in the captain's uniform stepped back, hand not dropping down to the handgun in his weapon's holster, knowing the safety flap would slow him. He glanced back to his sergeant, who was cursing and clawing to draw his pistol.

"That's not a Military Police vehicle, and you're not in a proper Military Police uniform," Bolan answered the first man, even as his right hand was freeing the Desert Eagle from its place on his hip. The move was lightning fast and smooth.

The gunman had out his Browning, but cursed as he stared down the huge black tunnel of the .44 Magnum pistol's barrel.

The Desert Eagle thundered like the voice of a god, and

the man dressed as a sergeant flew backward down the steps. People on the street screamed as a body with half a head smacked the sidewalk.

Bolan continued his discourse. "Also, the British army wouldn't send a captain to pick up an offending officer. He'd get two sergeants, the driver and the arresting officer."

Whether the rank officer was phony or real, it didn't matter to Bolan. The captain was on the attack, hands reaching out to peel the huge Israeli pistol from the Executioner's hand. Bolan flicked the safety lever on and let the man have the pistol without incident, slipping free.

"Also, even if a captain was sent to pick up another officer of equal rank, he wouldn't be talking on his cell phone. All the paperwork would have been done, or he wouldn't have been on his way in the first place."

Unbalanced by the sudden passive strategy, the officer teetered on the step.

Bolan snapped a hard kick into the man's stomach, throwing him down the stairs in a clumsy tumble. Recovering his own balance, the Executioner drew his Beretta 93-R and aimed at the armed driver of the army car, flicking the selector switch to tri-burst. He hosed the windshield and roof with a dozen rounds as the driver tried to take aim and revved the engine, preparing for a fast getaway.

After the salvo of slugs, the car merely idled forward, rear-ending a van.

The driver's corpse was slumped over the steering wheel, perforated with the 9 mm slugs that managed to pierce the body of the sedan.

"Is that good enough deductive reasoning for you?" Bolan asked. He aimed at the thug who had hold of his Desert Eagle. The Briton was busy trying to figure out how to shoot the gun as his Executioner leveled the Beretta.

"Fuck you!" the man growled, throwing the Desert Eagle.

Bolan felt the gun bounce off his shoulder as he leaned out of the way. The Executioner took a deep breath, realizing that this man wasn't going to surrender. He fired a 3-round burst into the head of the killer as he went for his side arm.

The Executioner bent, picked up the .44 Magnum pistol, inspected it, then holstered it after giving it a clean bill of health. He watched Dean and Goh take off in Goh's Jaguar.

The soldier, however, wouldn't be joining them.

Not until he delivered more judgment.

THE SIGHT OF THE BIG MAN strolling into the nightclub was enough to get most of the patrons moving out of the way and give Jacob Barrett a heart flutter.

In his long flapping black coat, the stranger cut through the crowd, his face a hard, craggy mask of cold fury. He was tall, but not too tall, and not too heavily muscled. If he hadn't entered with a kick of the door and a purpose of step, he would have come in unnoticed.

Instead, he stormed toward Barrett, eyes locked on him, homing in like some kind of missile. Barrett shifted uneasily behind his table at the club.

Hull, his bodyguard, rose to greet the stranger, but the flash of a fist swept across his face, the sound of a jaw bursting like a shattering bottle on concrete. Barrett's hands reached under his jacket, but a pistol was in the big, dark stranger's hand, leveled at a spot just over his heart.

"You pull that pistol, you deliver my message with your coffin," Mack Bolan said, moving the selector of his Beretta 93-R to 3-round-burst mode for extra emotional impact.

Barrett froze under the Executioner's aim. "What message do you want me to send?"

Bolan fished a card out of his breast pocket with his left hand, then threw it on the table. "I borrowed this number from the man he sent to kill Head. He can call me on it."

Barrett nodded, swallowing hard. "Who do I give the message to?"

Bolan gave the table a kick, wedging it harder against Barrett's gut, pinning him in his booth. "You know who I'm talking about. If not, then think of the second scariest person you've ever met."

Etienne De Simmones, Barrett thought, eyes widening.

"That's who," Bolan growled as he recognized the spark of realization crossing Barrett's face. It was a good piece of psychological warfare that left most of Bolan's enemies off guard when he anticipated their racing thoughts and fears. Simple reactions, though, were so easy to read, giving the master infiltrator total command of role camouflage, a weapon he'd used to hide among and sow confusion against his enemies across countless campaigns.

Again, the bar owner squirmed as Bolan leaned into him. "Don't forget. Call him. Have him talk to me."

Bolan turned and walked out. He left Barrett too frightened to do anything but pick up the card with a scrawled number on one side.

KEVIN GOH HAD WANTED to accompany Mack Bolan, but the soldier made it known he was going to make the tour of London's underworld by himself. He told Goh and Dean to hole up and stay put, and keep an ear on the cloned cell phone that Bolan made.

The technology was illegal, and Melissa Dean looked embarrassed at the ease with which the Executioner was able to use a couple of attachments from his laptop to make the duplicate. Bolan simply shrugged.

"Modern technology," Bolan said.

Having the two phones on one line gave them a relatively hard to trace form of communication. As long as their batteries lasted.

Bolan lowered his glasses after scouting out the restaurant. It was mobbed up like a fortress, and though it gave the appearance of being busy, he knew full well that the men inside were there on triad business. There were too many men, not enough women, and all the faces were grim and Chinese.

Two guys out front gave the impression that they were not just doormen. It might have had to do with the brace of machine pistols making their jackets look lumpy, and the fact that they wore sunglasses at night. Bolan almost found the situation comical. With the Colt SMG, it would have been an easy shot to take them both down in a heartbeat, but he was going for rattling cages, not racking up a lot of hits.

He lowered the scoped submachine gun and used the cover of shadows to get to the parking lot.

There, one of the younger, rawer triad recruits was earning his bones manning the lot, performing valet services. When he saw the long lean form of the Executioner stroll up, he caught a glimpse of Bolan's slung Colt before the long flaps of his coat swung shut. He paused, confused. That hesitation saved the young man's life, for the moment at least, giving Bolan a chance to get close and deliver a stunning knee to the gut. As the triad punk folded over Bolan's leg, he caught an elbow between his shoulder blades and dropped to the tarmac in a numb, coughing heap.

Knowing that would attract the attention of the guys out front in the space of a few seconds, Bolan hauled the kid to his feet and kept walking, pulling him along, cutting to the side entrance and pounding on the door.

Bolan stepped to one side, and the slit in the door snapped open. The eyes on the other side could see only a coughing, wheezing young man, clutching his gut and trying to avoid vomiting all over his designer jeans. As the heavy door swung open, Bolan shoved the kid in hard and followed him before slamming the door shut.

The guard on the other side backed up, mouth open in shock. Bolan hauled out the Colt and rapped the guard in the temple with the butt of the gun's pistol grip. The triad soldier quivered with the impact, then sank to the floor before he could utter a sound. Bolan let the Colt drop on its sling, and patted down the two men for their weapons. He was rewarded with a Heckler & Koch MP-5 K machine pistol and a MAC-11.

He gripped the MAC-11 in his left fist, stuffed the MP-5 K in the crook of his left elbow and fished out a card from his pocket. He poked a steel throwing spike through the center of the card and had his message ready to send.

The message was simple. "Ask De Simmones why you bled tonight."

The Executioner peered around the corner, still in the shadows. There was a man standing in the center of the restaurant. He was talking about the resolution of a conflict between two groups over heroin running.

Bolan targeted the speaker, hauled off and threw the spike, catching the man in the belly. He fell backward, coughing and gripping the steel that had rammed into him.

Men rose, guns drawn, but the MP-5 K was already falling into Bolan's right hand, the MAC-11 in his left fist ripping a swathe of destruction and confusion among the assembled mobsters. By the time the MAC-11 ran dry, the MP-5 K was laying out a sheet of lead and Bolan backed toward the door to the parking lot.

The chatterbox dropped from Bolan's hand and he went for the Colt under his jacket. The exit door he was sidestepping toward thundered open. The two men from out front stormed in, but Bolan was already on the case with the Colt in his left hand, holding down the trigger and perforating the pair of gunmen before they could even evaluate what was going on inside the restaurant. Bolan returned his attention to his back trail, even as he retreated into the lot.

As he was through the doorway, Bolan reached into his harness and yanked a grenade. The pin came off with the pull, and he rolled the grenade to the door, which was filled with men struggling to chase their attacker but getting caught up in themselves.

The explosion wasn't a lethal one. It was a simple stun-shock grenade, but rolled among the legs of men in a cramped hallway, at such close quarters, the thundering report of its detonation threw the men around like dolls, squirting bodies out the doorway. One man screamed as the heavy hunk of metal that used to be the detonator lodged in his thigh. Bolan simply crossed the street as he pulled a second grenade and lobbed it back toward the lot.

By the time he was across the road, the bomb had deto-nated, setting off more cries of pain and confusion. Bolan slipped behind the wheel of his BMW and fired up the en-gine.

Etienne De Simmones was not going to be a popular man by the end of this evening.

THE ROW OF BASEBALL BATS on the wall was cold comfort to Shamus Drake. His storefront full of gambling machines had a veneer of semirespectability. He used his operation to keep tabs on the underworld, occasionally assisting his old com-mander, Etienne De Simmones, whenever he needed an ear to the ground, or matériel scrounged up.

If it had wheels and wasn't on fire, Drake could get it for you. He had a car lot just down the block. He owned it through a couple of cutouts, two Jamaicans who needed le-gitimate jobs in exchange for their residency in London.

The bell above the door jingled as it was thrown open. Drake glanced up at the pair of terrified-looking, sweating men.

"What the hell are you doing here?" he asked.

"The lot—" one began.

"Big guy!" the other sputtered.

"Idiots," Drake muttered, reaching for his baseball bat.

He opened the door and stepped out onto the sidewalk, only to see the street awash in golden light glowing from a couple of blocks down. A man was walking toward him, backlit, tall and powerful, a pillar of muscle in black holding something in his hands. The sound of a gas tank exploding shook the air.

Drake froze at the sound of the detonation, midswing on the bat.

The gun sputtered quietly, and the wood of the slugger splintered, an invisible force ripping it from his grip and tossing it down the sidewalk. He looked back at his weapon, then at the wraith advancing on him.

The man glowered at Drake, leveling the Colt SMG, the M-203 grenade launcher under it looking like a tunnel. Now he knew why his dealership was in flames, and he also guessed why the gun was being aimed right at his face.

"Ask Etienne De Simmones why you're burning tonight," the man said.

The Executioner stuffed a card into Drake's breast pocket, gave his cheek a gentle slap to make sure he wasn't in shock and walked off into the darkness.

CARMINE TURICCI TOOK a puff on his cigar as he listened to the urgent phone call. Someone was making a tour of London, and they were hitting sites that the Organized Crime division would have loved to look into. Most of them were regular local mobsters, but the Chinese were hit too.

Someone walked into their big meeting, dropped a calling card into the gut of the guest speaker, then walked away after emptying ninety rounds of automatic fire and two grenades into whoever was trying to chase him.

There was a full-on investigation by the metropolitan police, but they were trying to deal with two shootings at different city hospitals, and the killing of three men on the steps of one of their own police stations.

A force of nature was sweeping across London, and Turicci knew enough to smell disaster.

Thunder suddenly crashed in the hallway and a body tumbled through the door, most of its face blown off in a gory blob of pulped brain and stringy muscle. For a second, Turicci stared in surprise, then his hand went for the Walther in the top drawer of his desk.

That's when the bogeyman turned the corner into the room, Desert Eagle leading the way, as big as hell, cutting the air in front of him.

Turicci didn't even get a warning. The Magnum pistol launched its payload into his forearm. Bones snapped and tendons were severed. The London Mafia boss pulled his arm back, his hand twitching and hanging at a sickening angle to the rest of his limb.

"You shot my arm off!" Turicci wailed.

The Executioner didn't speak. He walked to the desk, rammed a knife with a card at the end of it into the blotter and pivoted in time to turn two of the mobsters' men into stew with three quick .44 Magnum judgments.

"You know who I am?" Bolan asked Turicci.

"Oh God…yes…"

"You know the program then. I'll see myself out."

Bolan walked halfway through the office, to the door, and stopped. He turned, pointing an accusing finger at Turicci. "I'll be back later. We have old times to catch up on."

Turicci felt a hot rush of urine, dropping back into his chair. He looked at the knife rammed into his desk and reached for the card, plucking it off the edge.

Scrawled on it were a short message and a phone number.

"Ask Etienne De Simmones why your home's littered with bodycocks."

A circle and crosshairs were the only signature.

Turicci made his own sign of the cross, tears staining his cheeks.

THE PHONE CLATTERED down on its hook and Terry Waddington's hands shook as he heard the news. De Simmones had been phoning around, warning that someone was stalking through London, looking for a link to him.

And instead of being told to keep his mouth shut, the deal was that he let this stranger know that De Simmones was willing to do a meet and greet, or at least talk over the phone.

Waddington heard the credentials on this mystery man, Matt Cooper. He'd put down Vincent Black and Rory MacKinnon. Those two were hard men, and they didn't travel with lightweights. Waddington was no pushover in his own right, though. He walked behind his desk and opened his drawer.

The big Ruger GP-100 inside was a reassuring piece of hardware. The last of the great .357 Magnum revolver innovations before the rise of the autopistol, it was a six-shooter that was as strong as any handgun ever made, and quite accurate. The weight of the gun was comforting, enough to shatter bone if necessary.

He pulled out the big gun and flipped open the cylinder. All six fire holes were filled, and each of the rounds was fresh and live. No imperfections on the base of them, nothing to indicate that they would jam.

Waddington swung the cylinder closed and smiled as the gun came into battery with the reassuring clank of heavy steel connecting. A second click drew his attention.

"Put it down and turn around slowly," the Executioner ordered softly.

Waddington closed his eyes, his hands grown weak. It felt

like his bones dissolved into gelatin, and only the power of fear kept him standing upright. An icy chill washed over him as he set the revolver on top of his desk and turned to look down the barrel of a massive .44 Magnum pistol.

"Who called you?" Mack Bolan asked him.

"It was Etienne De Simmones. He was calling around to leave messages with his people."

"What message?" Bolan pressed.

"He wants to talk," Waddington answered.

"Big coincidence. Here."

The ex-SAS man took the card stuffed between his fingers. He looked down at it and recognized the cell-phone number.

"Where did you get this from?" Waddington asked.

Bolan touched the tip of Waddington's chin with the Desert Eagle and locked eyes with the man. "I got it from a dead man whose brains were splashed on the sidewalk in front of a police station. Now it's mine," he said.

Waddington sat back on the desk, numb and cold. His fingertips brushed against the butt of the Ruger.

"You killed a friend of mine, asshole," Waddington growled.

"De Simmones is killing innocent people, and he killed the sister of a friend of mine," Bolan countered. "Anyone who wants to put up a fight, I'm not going to deny them their chance to die a fool."

Waddington swung the Ruger, but the Desert Eagle that was shoved in his face detonated with a blinding flash and his hearing disappeared behind a wall of ringing agony. He didn't think that he'd survived, but when he opened his burning eyes, he was looking at the ceiling, one ear feeling like it had been kicked in by a mule. He couldn't feel his shoulder or arm. He clumsily raised his remaining hand to feel his muzzle-blasted face, and then the gory, spongy mass that used to be the bone and muscle of his joint.

Waddington coughed, vomiting up bile, but a hand pressed to his jaw, turning him on his side.

"You don't die until you deliver my message. Got that?" Bolan asked.

Waddington nodded weakly.

"I've called an ambulance for you. Call De Simmones."

With that, the tall stranger turned and left the bleeding former SAS commando on the floor.

11

Inspector Melissa Dean didn't like sitting on the sidelines, not when she had her own abilities. As long as Matt Cooper was busy making life hell for Etienne De Simmones, she was going to see why her sister was murdered.

That meant finding out why Basil Carrington was dead in a hotel room, possibly killed by an untraced neurotoxin.

No real evidence existed to the mystery poison, but bodies were stacking up like cordwood around the city, so there had to be some reason for it. Waves of attackers and killers were popping out of every nook and cranny, eager for a shot at the man who claimed to be a Boston cop.

That meant, for the sake of her sanity, she had to know what conspiracy her sister died exposing. Carrington's apartment was easy enough to break into, and from the looks of things, Dean was afraid that the Ripper's crew had already been through it. But, on closer inspection, the disarray of paperwork and the litter of fast-food cartons only bespoke the lifestyle of a single man with more important things on his mind than cleaning and hygiene, rather than the roughshod search of an apartment.

Dean wasn't sure if she was double-checking the Beretta on her hip because she feared rats and large cockroaches, or if she was anticipating that a cleaning crew would come in and give her hell at any moment. Either way, the gun was cleared for a clean draw.

Carrington wasn't a man of means. His newspaper wasn't large. It was run mostly through donations, and the hard work of fellow conspiracy theorists who invested their madness and time into spreading the fear of those in power. Printing costs were low in the age of the corner photocopy store.

She looked at the computer in the corner on a table. It was a laptop, pressed into service as the center of Carrington's desktop publishing program. She walked over to it and wondered how much the paranoid man would really have committed to disk, especially considering what she knew of theories about spy programs and killer applications.

The laptop was connected to a phone line, and she knew for sure that this was a dead end. Carrington was a man distrustful of the government, and allowing a modem into his computer meant that he was allowing the powers that be to watch his every move. There had to be something else. She only had to be methodical in her search for it.

She checked the obvious places first. Under sinks. Under drawers. She opened the closet, and of all places, it was the only place in order.

That set off her alarm bells immediately. She kneeled and moved shoe boxes around. They were heavy, and she noticed that the ones on the bottom were held together by clear packing tape.

Bingo, she thought.

She took the lid off a double shoe box and discovered another laptop, this one with flash memory drives in a box on top of it. She contemplated taking the laptop with her, but instead, she took it out, powered it up and ran a search for documents in the drive.

Except for help files, there was nothing but some Internet porn.

Of course.

He simply wrote whatever he had onto the flash drives.

There were a couple dozen of them, literally gigabytes of potential information. She'd need a good system to look at them, and remembered Matt Cooper's very powerful personal notebook computer.

That should be able to crack anything on the flash drives. She had pocketed them and gotten up when she heard scraping at the front door of the apartment.

The Beretta was in her hand, safety snapped off without a conscious thought. She was a little frightened at how smoothly and surely she was able to draw and ready the pistol, but that disappeared at the reassuring thought that she was well-armed, and she was ready for whatever came through that door.

The door opened.

"Make it quick," a voice grunted.

There was another grunt of affirmation, and a body appeared in the door of the bedroom, holding a weapon in both hands. Dean was crouched low, in the shadows behind the bed, her Beretta gripped tightly. Heavy footfalls went to the closet, but as soon as he reached it, there was a hissed curse.

"Someone's been here!" the intruder rasped.

He was in midturn when he had to have caught Dean's shadow out of the corner of his eye. She lunged forward, landing on one shoulder, her Beretta pointing out ahead of her. The gunman swept the mattress. Bullets pierced the heavy padding, snapping through coils and ripped out the side of the mattress, slamming into the wall where she'd been a heartbeat before.

Gunfire turned the tiny bedroom into the center of a drum solo committed by a mad god. Slugs smashing into the mattress spit up fluff and flotsam of torn and burned cloth. Dean's return fire struck the searcher dead center, knocking him back into the closet, hard. One booted heel smashed through the keyboard of the laptop and kicked it under the bed in a wild tumble. By the time he crashed onto the floor, auto-weapon flying from lifeless fingers, Dean had scrambled to her feet, looking back to see how close she was to being torn to pieces by the thug.

A voice calling out from the living room. "Angus!"

The detective brought up her Beretta, leveling it at the doorway. A body appeared for a brief second, and Dean tripped the trigger, but the enemy was gone, her 9 mm slug spent uselessly. Pressing herself tight against the wall, she kept the doorway covered.

"Angus!" came a second cry.

He wasn't going to get an answer, and a burst of automatic fire tore into the drywall that Dean was tucked against. She recoiled, curling away from the advancing sweep of destruction.

If his bullets could punch through, so could hers, she figured. She angled out the Beretta once his fire stopped and worked the trigger until the gun emptied itself. Her hand plunged to pull the heavy-caliber Kahr from its hiding space and she stuffed the hot Beretta back into its holster.

That's when she heard the clunk of something heavy and metallic landing on the hardwood floor. "Burn in hell, asshole!" came the snarl out in the hallway.

A second burst of full-auto fire tore through the wall, ripping chunks free and producing a hole the size of a pie plate that the British detective could see her enemy through. She memorized his face in that instant, just before he dashed out the front door of the apartment.

A gout of smoke vomited up from the floor on the other side of the hole, and Dean swung into the doorway to see the floor burning. Flames lapped up, waist deep, and clouds of smoke crawled their way into the bedroom. Dean turned to the window, knowing that if she didn't get to fresh air, she'd be caught in the conflagration and suffocated long before her flesh felt the searing flame of the out of control fire.

The window was locked, and she hammered to pry the painted-over latch loose. It didn't budge.

Her eyes stung from the acrid smoke reaching to consume her.

The heavy weight of the Kahr in her fist caught her attention. The gun was small, flat and sleek, but it weighed a considerable amount, and it was made entirely of steel. With its weight, and the safety of its trigger, she could use it as a hammer without putting a bullet through her own belly by accident.

A solid rap with the butt of the gun moved the latch a quarter of the distance. She swung and struck again, this time missing and putting her whole hand through the window. Dean winced as she felt stings in her flesh and looked at the dripping blood that was seeping up her sleeve. She turned her wrist to see a slender shard of glass poking into her forearm.

"Bloody hell," she grated, trying her best to balance caution for her injured arm and speed against the racing smoke. She got her arm out and pulled the length of glass from it. No fresh blood spurted from a severed artery, but there was plenty of the red fluid covering her hand from cuts and slices. Nothing that would prove fatal, unless she spent too much time ogling it and breathed in the oxygen-denying smoke.

Dean looked around and slashed at the old threadbare sheets with the broken glass, wrapping a strip of cloth around her hand and wrist. She winced as she applied pressure, but knew that if she got out, she could get help later. She made a half-face mask for herself from another strip of bed sheet and tied it around her nose and jaw to filter out the smoke.

It wouldn't last long.

Flames were spreading into the room, and Dean needed to get out through the window fast. She saw the pillow, then looked to the window. Grabbing the cushion, she swung it against the panes of glass and punched, using the barrel of the Kahr to add to the force of her blows into the softness of the cushion. Glass shattered and tumbled away. If the shards cut anything, it was the unfeeling padding that she had clutched in her hands.

Sweeping the pistol and the pillow along the frame, she knocked the last of the glass free. Tendrils of smoke swirled down and poured out through the two holes she made, and Dean followed it, reaching for fresh air.

The ledge was narrow, and she was thirty-five feet in the air.

The only way down would be to find a pipe to shimmy, and there was none visible. Looking around, there was almost nothing that she had that could give her enough leverage to get to the ground without breaking her bones. Heat flashed on one of her legs, signaling to her that the flames were closing around her.

Ahead of her, she saw a lamp post. It was a ten-foot jump, and it was about ten feet below her. If she missed, she'd hit the middle of the road and probably spray out a fan of blood when she struck the ground, breaking bones and rupturing internal organs.

Even if she grabbed the lamp, she'd end up hurting something.

She decided it was better than burning to death.

Dean snaked out onto the ledge and stepped to one side. Flames and smoke licked out of the window, literally on her heels, and she shied away from the sudden jet furnace. The fire fed on oxygen, breathing it in and growing in power.

Dean's foot slipped as a renewed flame roared out the window and she dropped off the ledge. Only her hands managed to grip it and she found herself hanging over the ledge below her. Her arms ached and her fingers burned as gravity pulled her downward.

Mentally, she measured the distance down to the next ledge. Fifteen feet.

She let go, clawing her arms and fingers forward as she

was sucked down toward the ground. Hitting the second ledge gave her an education in what hitting a brick wall felt like. Her arms stung, pricks of pain running all along them as her legs kicked freely in the wind.

Not the most graceful of falls.

But she'd survived. She looked to the ground. She had about fifteen feet to drop, and it was to hard concrete, but the sidewalk wasn't quite so dangerous now. Not if she cushioned herself for the impact.

Relaxing her muscles, she slithered backward off the ledge and dropped down. Her legs were bent, but pain shocked up through them nonetheless. She tumbled to one side. Her muscles felt ripped and raw, and her thighs were aflame with agony.

But she was able to feel her toes and fingertips. Bones didn't seem to have broken. And she could stand, albeit with considerable effort.

She hobbled to Goh's Jaguar and got in, resting in the driver's seat for a moment. The cushions were comfortable, soothing her sore body against the aches she'd just acquired.

She realized that it was the second time she'd killed a man, and this time was just as easy as the first. No doubts, no worries, no fears.

She realized sometimes, you had to get bloody to take on those who didn't value life.

It was like Goh had said. You had to balance what mattered. Innocent lives, or their murderers.

There was no doubt in Dean's mind that the gunman she'd killed was a coldhearted murderer who had burned down unarmed bystanders before in the name of whatever deluded duty he aspired to. His death wouldn't weigh on her as much as the death of her sister, or the injuries of the people storming out of the apartment building in the middle of the night, trying to keep their wits about them as their homes burned. His death wouldn't even begin to matter anymore.

Dean could see where Matt Cooper had those moments of haunted loneliness—not from being a lone-wolf killer, but from being a man who was surrounded by death that could strike out at the vulnerable, the weak, the harmless he was devoted to protecting.

The Rippers had no qualms with attacking innocent people.

Dean felt better, knowing she had no qualms about putting the Rippers in the ground.

Yuri Astonitev was being kept up to date on the war tearing through London's meaner streets. So far, nobody had reacted to him, and he wondered what sparked the network under Etienne De Simmones and the Italian and Chinese Mobs to bristle and take up arms in preparation for a war.

"Two more police reports coming in, sir," Sergei Zelikov spoke up, breaking Astonitev's reverie. "Turicci's household has reported gunfire, and a used-car dealership turned into an inferno."

"Drake's?" Astonitev asked.

"That's what the police assume," Zelikov replied. "Of course, we've dealt with Drake, and we know for sure."

Astonitev sat back. "We're behind too much security here. There is no way—"

A brief explosion of gunfire sounded behind the storehouse. The ex-KGB agent whirled at the sound. "What the hell are they doing?"

"Dying," Zelikov shouted. He reached for the pistol he kept under his jacket, then stopped.

"Dying…then why aren't you getting your gun?" Astonitev snapped. "We have to defend ourselves!"

"The only thing you have to do is ask Etienne De Simmones why you're going to lose a couple million pounds in contraband," a voice said from behind.

Astonitev whirled, going for his gun, but a knifelike chop

cut across his shoulder, numbing the limb and making any fine motor skill like a gun draw impossible. The Russian *mafiya* boss struggled.

The man behind him was big, but lean and swift, one knotted arm blocking the Russian's opening punch. He was dressed all in black, and weapons bristled from a harness he wore across his broad, powerful chest. With a lunge, Astonitev grabbed at the Beretta in the man's shoulder harness, twisting and pulling it free.

It was the last thing the Mob boss ever did. The muzzle of the Desert Eagle rammed deep into the Russian's stomach muscles, and when the gun couldn't move any more, the trigger squeezed tight. The hammer dropped and a 240-grain boattail hollowpoint round blew through Astonitev's torso in one body-wrenching blast.

Numbed fingers released the handle of the Beretta in the Executioner's holster, and the wounded man stumbled backward for three steps. He put both hands to the hole in his belly and looked down.

Entrails wrapped around his leg from where they'd been blown out of his back. His knees weakened, and a heartbeat later, he tumbled lifelessly to the floor.

"You could have shot me," Bolan said to Zelikov.

"You'd have killed me."

Bolan nodded. "You know there is a message I want you to send."

Zelikov thought about it for a moment. "That is correct. Etienne De Simmones. I will send the message for you."

Zelikov shuddered as the big man in black disappeared.

BOLAN ANSWERED on the second ring. "What's happening?" he said immediately.

"Melissa smells like an ashtray," Kevin Goh said. "She nearly got torched at Carrington's apartment."

Bolan winced at the thought. "Is she okay otherwise?"

"Some cuts, but nothing that severed a major vein or artery. We've got it all wrapped up nice and pretty," Goh explained.

"So do you have something for me?"

"She found a stack of flash drives containing notes and layouts for issues of *The Clarion*. We think. We'll wait until you show up."

"I've still got business," Bolan said. "Sign onto my laptop." He gave Goh the password. "Simple enough, and you'll have access to everything except communications programming."

"You sure?"

"Positive. I need information, and you can do it. Was Dean followed?" Bolan asked.

"I don't think so, but we've got good locks on this place, we've got the extra guns you gave us, and I have three loaded shotguns ready to deliver some additional mayhem if something comes by."

"And nobody else knows about where you'd be?" Bolan asked.

"Nope," Goh replied.

"Good. I'll call when I'm coming in. Hang up before someone tries tracing this phone."

The phone disconnected.

Dean had disobeyed Bolan's request and gone out seeking information, and nearly been incinerated for her troubles. That's what he was afraid of, that reckless streak. Bolan had managed to tame himself, and while he didn't doubt that the lady detective was being as careful as she could have been, he knew that recklessness often led to deadly results.

Bolan gunned the BMW and headed for a meeting with De Simmones's arms dealer.

KEVIN GOH POCKETED his phone. He checked to make sure that the shotgun he'd propped against the couch wouldn't topple when he sat down, and seated himself across from Melissa Dean, who sat barefoot and cross-legged on the floor, looking at the laptop. Her features were lit from below by the white screen of the computer.

She looked almost ethereal, ghostlike and beautiful. It was as if someone had carved her from crystal and polished her. Only the movement of her eyes dispelled the illusion of her being a statue. She brushed a lock of hair from her forehead and looked up at him.

"What, Kevin?" she asked.

"Sorry, didn't mean to stare," Goh replied. His cheeks flushed and he felt stupid. He knew that their friendship wasn't like that. He was loyal to her, and he cared about her. Such dreamy-eyed thoughts only detracted from the fact that they were two people who could work together and not give in to animal passions.

Dean nodded. "Listen, I nearly got killed tonight, my sister is dead and I'm finding out that there's things my government is doing to kill innocent people. I'm not in the mood for pussyfooting around and hiding away my feelings."

Goh tilted his head.

"Thank you for being here. I'm sorry I got you into this, but something tells me that even if we were going to shoot the queen, you'd be backing me up," Dean continued. "You'd be there to protect me no matter what."

Goh looked down at the floor. "Melissa…"

"And through it all, even though you'd be dying to say it on the inside, your sense of honor wouldn't allow you to put into words the feelings you're hiding because you would be afraid of offending me."

Goh sighed. "Yes."

Dean took a step forward and slipped her arms around him, resting her head on his shoulder. His heart took a half-skip, then settled down. Her embrace wasn't one of passion, but of affection. She leaned against him, and he returned her warmth.

"Kevin, I can't thank you enough for sticking with me. I know I might seem like a brass-balled bitch," she whispered. Her lips brushed against his neck and Goh wrapped his arms around her, as much as to finally return the affection presented as to make sure he didn't tumble out of her grasp. "After losing so much, after almost losing my last chance to say this to you, I don't want to wait anymore, I have to tell you how I feel now. Thank you for being here. I couldn't ask for a better partner."

He whispered into her ear, "Melissa, I would feel dead to the world if you were gone."

"You won't lose me," Dean answered. "I'm going to be here. I have too much to live for."

"Revenge isn't a reason to live."

"But you are, my friend."

All they had to do was to survive the slings and arrows, the fire and brimstone of the coming hell storm, and they would come through on the other side.

It wasn't going to be easy. The bulk of the Beretta stuffed into Goh's waistband was a reminder of that.

Over two pounds of ugly metal hanging off him. What he once considered the epitome of Hong Kong action movie cool, was now a grim weight of reality. The weight of death tugging at his belt, letting him know that for now, every embrace, every moment of intimacy was cut off by the very solid reminder of death lurking in wait for them. He was furious at the sheet of violence that cut them off from each other.

Amid affection and anger, Goh held Dean tight.

He was afraid that if he let go, the world would fall apart.

12

The network that De Simmones had set up in London was being unraveled, piece by piece. De Simmones and Tern listened to the reports coming in, the calls being made, the accusations flying all evening. The Russians, the Italians and the Chinese weren't sitting still for the blood spilt on their account. They were throwing lead at his people.

The former SAS men at the tops of these organizations were able to hold off most of the attacks, although the Russian *mafiya*'s stable of ex-military men were making De Simmones sweat. He knew that when it came down to the line, he could hold his own against the other organizations. These were small reactions, minor hits, for show only, to make the other organizations see that they weren't weak.

Another thing burned and seethed like a gnawing parasite at De Simmones. He had lost a half dozen operations to the mystery man, Matt Cooper, in his rampage across London. The American was a one-man army that struck and faded, leaving blood and flame in his wake.

"Waddington is in the hospital. His men are either dead or in hiding," De Simmones reported to Tern.

The younger renegade adjusted a leather glove on his right hand, listening only halfheartedly.

"What about Carrington's apartment?" Tern asked. "Has that been taken care of?"

"We lost Angus, but Thompson followed the bird who dropped the hammer on him. He's waiting for some backup," De Simmones answered. "You're in charge now, so what do you think? Wait for Cooper to arrive?"

"Let's leave some bloodied messages for him," Tern responded. "Just like he left for us."

De Simmones smiled slyly. "Thompson, wait for my cue. We've got a couple of the lads loading up and coming your way."

"Make sure they're good," Tern commented. He picked up his own phone, then paused, regarding himself in the mirror. He had changed into a black suit, with matching leather gloves and short boots that ended in pointed tips. His hair was coiffed, and the only break in color was his shirt, a crushed velvet burgundy shirt with a pale cream tie down from the collar. He tightened the tie to make sure he looked perfect.

"You already look like a badass, Tern," De Simmones said.

Tern smirked, regarding the old boss out of the corner of his eye. "Thank you."

"Is that how you plan to greet Cooper?"

Tern pivoted on his heel so De Simmones could get a better look at the cut of the man's suit. Buttons opened, and he saw the butts of four Berettas poking out from under the side panels of the coat.

"I'm ready for anyone," Tern told him.

He lifted the phone and dialed the number from Waddington. He snapped his fingers, and De Simmones switched on the speaker.

"Talk fast," came the terse reply on the other end.

"Detective Matt Cooper?" Tern asked.

"The one and only. You must be De Simmones."

"No. I decided to take charge," Tern replied. "Etienne just doesn't have the spine to deal with a man like you. He's still here if you want to talk to him, but I think I'm the one you owe some apologies to."

"I'm not going to apologize for trying to put a bullet into you," Bolan said.

Tern chuckled. "It was such a clean crime scene too. A work of art."

"De Simmones let a freak like you play with his organization?" Bolan said.

Tern watched for the SAS vet's reaction. The old man stayed very still, not even a flinch of reaction crossing his features.

"He's choosing to stay out of our conversation."

"I'm not surprised. I get a little jumpy when I work with psychotic amateurs too."

"Amateur? I'm vetted. Blooded."

Bolan played cool. "Against who? Old ladies? Potato farmers with grudges?"

"You won't make me lose my control."

"You lost your control ages ago. When you started imitating Jack the Ripper, you lost any semblance of reality you ever held. You came up with the idea, right?" Bolan asked. "Get a girl to deliver some poison to your target, and then when you had your chance, kill her. Make it look like Jack the Ripper. Put your work in the headlines. No hiding the work you did for Mother England behind the *Official Secrets Act*. You'd be front page news. Hiding your real job, though, that was just the icing on the cake, the sweet stuff that made De Simmones think that it was an actual plan, something that—"

"Shut up!" Tern snapped. "I'm the man in control right now."

De Simmones heard his phone ring. It was Thompson's voice on the other end.

"The boys are here."

"Take out the coppers," De Simmones ordered. "Scorched earth."

"A pleasure," Thompson replied.

"Hear that, Cooper?" Tern asked. "You tried to get me to lose my control. But you lost your two friends. Ask Liam Tern why your friends are bleeding tonight!"

There was only a dial tone coming from the speakerphone.

"That'll show him," Tern said, turning and adjusting his jacket. He admired himself in the mirror, oblivious to the drone of the speaker box as De Simmones turned it off.

THE PHONE WARBLED and Goh picked it up first. Dean was still looking at the laptop.

"Get out now! They followed Dean!" Bolan said.

"Shit! Melissa!" Goh shouted.

Dean grabbed the box of flash drives, stuffing it into her purse. She ripped the last remaining drive from the back of the computer, tucking it into her pocket. Bolan's laptop lay there. "How much of his stuff should we save?"

"Forget the computer. They're coming to kill you!" Bolan said, anticipating the question.

Goh flipped one of the shotguns to Dean. She checked it over and looked to see if there was a round in the breech. She was still wearing her Beretta from before, loose rounds replacing the ammunition she'd expended.

Glass shattered and the wall near the window seemed to explode. Goh and Dean dived to the floor.

"We're boned," Goh muttered.

"Goh, I need an address!" Bolan shouted.

Goh spit back the address.

All the while, pieces of the safehouse walls rained down as heavy-caliber slugs tore apart brick and drywall. Goh hated cringing and curling up against the assault, but it was the only logical thing to do. He gripped his shotgun tightly in his free hand, looking around.

"I can be there in fifteen minutes," Bolan shouted. "Just survive."

"That was my plan," Goh stated. Something came through the wall and smacked him hard. The phone flew from his grip, skittering across the floor.

Wincing, he felt along his arm to find out where he'd been hit when a spray of blood blinded him. Goh gasped, blinking the hot stickiness out of his vision, when a hand grabbed him and pressed him flat to the floor. His hand was numb, and he still hadn't figured out what had hit him.

Dean's face hovered over his own, and she put her arm over him. "You got shot in the forearm!"

Goh tried to lift his arm, but Dean's weight on his biceps kept him from moving it.

"Don't lift anything!" Dean warned. "They're tearing this place apart."

"Bloody hell," Goh murmured. "Why do I feel like I've been kicked in the head?"

"That bruise where the phone hit you looks like a good reason," Dean told him. "I'm going to drag you. Hang on to your shotgun."

Squirming, Dean tugged him away from the center of the living room, putting most of the furniture in the safehouse between them and the incoming fire. The sofa shuddered as multiple slugs impacted it, but after going through a wall, the bullets didn't have much energy left.

As soon as they reached a position of safety in the front hall, the shooting stopped. Dean plucked the shotgun from Goh's hands.

The front door was suddenly kicked in by two men with guns. Goh rolled hard against the wall, the floor turning to splinters beneath him. Shotgun blasts thundered in the confined space, making his already aching head throb. His ears popped with each overpressure blast of 12-gauge cannonade.

He clawed for the Beretta with his left hand and got it free. With a snap of his thumb, he had the safety off and he saw that Dean had left the body of one of their attackers a seeping, gory mess on the doorstep. Rib bones glistened from where a salvo of buckshot tore away skin and muscle like the skin of an orange. The dead man's protective goggles stared sightlessly like a single, unblinking eye toward the night sky outside.

"One down," Goh said, groaning. He brought his legs up beneath him, gathering his balance.

"Stay down," Dean whispered. "You're hurt."

"You can't fight off an invasion of commandos by yourself."

"I can sure try," she answered.

Goh reached out, but could only rest the slide of his Beretta against her hip. She shrugged away, disappearing from him.

Dean moved halfway down the hall, then stopped and racked a fresh shell into the breech. The shotgun roared again. A body jerked violently, legs kicked up as a swarm of buckshot hammered into it. The corpse slumped onto the other wrecked form.

"Melissa!" Goh shouted.

Instinct took over and he checked behind him for possible new threats. A shadow loomed in the darkness, a red beam of light emanating from under an object in its hands. Goh swung his pistol as the red laser slashed down at him.

Goh rolled to one side. Bullets tore ragged shreds out of the wall he'd been slumped against. His side exploded with searing heat and pain shot through his entire body. Even as he curled against the pain, he triggered the Beretta, 9 mm rounds powered out the end, homing in on the looming form over him.

The muzzle-flash flickered like lightning. The spurts of light illuminated the falling machine gunner, his weapon jerked to the ceiling. Slugs sawed up and into the ceiling above them, splinters and chunks raining down on both of them. But the gunner wasn't in control of his weapon, his finger clenched tight in a dead man's grip, life pouring away as the spent brass poured out of the breech.

Goh coughed and tasted blood in his mouth, then shrugged to push along the floor. No telling who else might be coming in from behind, and he wasn't sure how much of the ammunition in his Beretta he'd used.

"Reload," Dean whispered. She knelt by his side, the shotgun aimed into the shadows at the other end of the dining room.

Goh rested the Beretta on his stomach and pulled a fresh magazine. "I got hit again."

"Where?" Dean asked.

"I dunno, but I can taste blood."

"Fuck me."

Goh managed a weak smile as he dumped the old clip and loaded in a fresh one. His arm hurt like hell, but he could still use it somewhat. "I would, but with this pressure I'm feeling a bit under."

"Can't be feeling that bad," Dean whispered.

Something moved in the corner of Goh's vision and he threw himself flat. He bumped his head, but gave himself a perfect line of sight on the living room. The looming intruder was caught in stark contrast as he tried coming through the window. It was a narrow fit, and he paused, the muzzle of his gun poking through the glass to protect him from getting cut.

Goh opened fire and blazed away with five rapid rounds. The attacker jolted and stumbled back out of sight, but Goh knew that it wasn't a good hit. The muzzle of the laser-sighted machine pistol swung into the window, without the gunner's body, and rounds bounced wildly off the walls and furniture.

Dean reacted instantly. Her shotgun boomed and an instant later, the machine pistol was a lump of gore-covered metal inside the windowsill. Outside, screams filled the air. Goh squinted and saw the remains of a hand wrapped around the enemy weapon's grip.

He looked to Dean, who busied herself sliding shells into the magazine of her shotgun.

"Try to make a break for—"

"Shut the hell up. We're fighting to the finish. I'm not giving you up. I lost Melanie, I'm not losing you, dammit!"

"Ain't that touching!" someone called from outside.

More machine-gun fire tore through the wall of the safehouse, and both Goh and Dean hugged the floor. A bullet plucked at Goh's shirt between his shoulder blades.

"Ah hell, we're getting murdered," Goh muttered. He knew Dean couldn't hear him over the cacophony. The only consolation was that he was going to die next to his partner.

EVEN IF THE EXECUTIONER hadn't been given the address of the safehouse, the sound of the SAW would have drawn him to it like a moth to a flame. However, this flame was going to receive a visit from a moth in a blacksuit made of bullet- and flame-resistant fibers, and a harness for assorted weapons and spare ammunition. Bolan stomped on the gas pedal and swung his BMW toward the machine gunner, a stocky man with thick and powerful arms.

At the sound of the car's engine, the shooter whirled. He swept the hood of Bolan's rental. Gouges and holes tore throughout its length, some slugs skidding up into the windshield, forcing the warrior to duck behind the dashboard. In the moment he dived for cover, he knew that he'd lost the gunman.

Bolan heard the clatter of the heavy weapon off the grille and up the hood of the vehicle. The frame of the twenty-pound weapon, aided by momentum, hammered through the glass and clipped him in the right biceps and elbow. Pain shot from that area, but not enough to signal a crippling injury. He stomped on the brakes and brought the BMW to a halt.

It was time to go EVA, and he pushed open the passenger-side door, only to have it kicked back into his face as he lunged out. Stunned briefly, he tried to hold the door shut, but the stocky little gunman pulled the door open and grabbed at him. Bolan's mind cleared and he speared his hand toward the Ripper agent's gun hand. That deflected the gunman's aim, a 9 mm bullet meant for his head instead slammed into the dashboard.

The machine gunner's compact musculature made him enormously powerful, and he tore Bolan from the car as if the big soldier were a child. At the last moment, Bolan kicked against the vehicle's door frame, giving himself leverage to somersault and twist out of the grip of the bulldog-built ex-commando. That move popped him free and gave him more room as a second bullet chased after him.

Bolan knew there was no time to draw a pistol. It was up close and personal.

He folded both legs tight, building up the force to spring against the Ripper's machine gunner, then plowed into the stout man. It was like hitting a brick wall. The shooter had twenty pounds on Bolan, and arms like an ape, which immediately crashed down in unison on his back. The double impact dropped Bolan to his knees.

The soldier wrapped his arm around the bulldog's waist, squeezing tight and lifting him. That extra twenty pounds, all muscle, quadrupled as his broad-shouldered opponent twisted and squirmed, sending all his weight in multiple directions at once. Bolan grimaced, dug his hands into the guy's hips and pushed him off against the side of the house. The machine-gun-riddled brickwork collapsed under the collision between man and damaged stone.

Bolan kicked the gunner in the forearm, snapping the bone

like a twig and making him drop his Browning. Another kick swung lower, catching the man between the legs. That made him sit up and cough. A sickly retching sound boiled out of his throat, but Bolan followed up with a hard knee to the side of the man's skull, which twisted his head.

"You were at the alley," Bolan growled. He grabbed a fist-ful of the man's collar, and pulled the Desert Eagle, screwing it under his jaw. "Talk fast or die slow."

"About what?" Tom Carlton asked, blood flowing freely from his wrecked face.

"The Ripper's name. Where he and De Simmones are hiding. Now."

"The police are coming from all this shooting. I shot the hell out of your engine. You can't give me a proper torture."

Bolan drew back the Desert Eagle. "I'll shoot you through the gut and out your spine. With a broken back, you'll be easy loving in prison. If your entrails are ever repaired enough for you to be out of a hospital bed."

Carlton's eyes widened. Bolan pressed the front sight of the Desert Eagle against his abdomen for brutal emphasis.

"I told you…talk fast or die slow."

"Liam Tern. That's the Ripper. He's second in command, maybe took over from De Simmones because you've been bolloxing up his affairs."

"Where are they?"

"At an old waypoint in the Maginot Line."

"That's not convincing enough," Bolan said.

"Honest! There'd been new construction in the fifties and sixties, during the cold war. They built facilities even deeper under the old fortifications."

"How does an old SAS vet know about it and have access to it?"

"The same way you Americans have old Continuity of Government bases stumbled upon…and a little cash to the few people who do know. A little cash and services rendered."

"Blood spilled to pay for a headquarters," Bolan said.

Bolan shoved Carlton to the ground. "Where is that spot on the line?"

The muzzle of the Desert Eagle rose to the machine gunner's face.

The killer smirked. "It's near the old fort of Immerhoff. What do you think you can do, though? Tern will have a small army ready for you by the time you get there. An army of men as good, maybe better than me—" The Ripper cohort made a sudden lunge.

Bolan pulled the trigger and Carlton's face disappeared.

"Dean! Goh!" Bolan called.

"Here!" Dean called out.

"Almost here," Goh added.

Bolan looked to see the lady detective holding up her partner. Both stood on shaky legs, tattered and beaten. Dean was drenched with blood, but Goh looked the weaker, his already pale face gone porcelain in pallor.

"Melissa, Kevin?"

"The Jaguar… We need to get Kevin to a hospital. He's been shot."

"Twice…my arm, and my side."

Bolan stopped to retrieve his war bag from the BMW.

A shadow moved in the darkness, and the red line of a laser poked through the haze and smoke. The Executioner cut behind his car, flipping up both the Desert Eagle and the Beretta in one smooth motion. The last attacker snarled a warning, but the words were lost in the combined crash and thunder of dual pistols smashing the silence and his body with thunder and lead.

Another of the Ripper's agents lay pulped and bleeding on the sidewalk in front of the house.

Bolan jogged over to Dean and Goh and slipped his arm under Goh's other shoulder. "How's your breathing?"

"It's fine, but my side hurts like hell and I bit my tongue."

"I'm no medic, but it sounds like something grazed your ribs. A small fracture maybe, but the bones did the job they're supposed to—protect the lungs."

The three people made it to the Jaguar. Goh was placed in the back seat, and Dean took shotgun, literally, while Bolan slid behind the wheel.

"He'll be okay?" Dean asked, sounding worried.

"He'll be fine," Bolan answered. "But we can't hang around to answer questions."

"Damn it, damn it, damn it," Goh mumbled.

"Save your breath," Dean said soothingly.

"Listen, I have a friend in France. He'll be able to hook you up with anything you need. He's ex-Foreign Legion…" Goh told them. "His name is Lewis Smythe."

"Don't talk like you're dying," Dean told him.

Goh held her hand with his good one. "I'm not, I'm just not going to be running around for a while. But I'm not dead yet."

The car clipped a pothole, and Goh coughed up some blood. The cop paled even further, and then he slumped, grip loosening on Dean's hand.

"Fucker," Dean said, her face hard.

Bolan listened to Dean curse as he continued to race to the hospital.

13

The Executioner pulled the Jaguar away from the hospital, amid complaints and cries from the emergency-room staff. Melissa Dean sat quietly in the shotgun seat, thinking about Kevin Goh and his injuries. Worry wrinkled her brow and her silence was almost a solid thing, something Bolan didn't want to disturb.

He had to worry about getting to France and being able to fight. His war bag was not going to make it through customs on the ferry, and it certainly wasn't going to pass through airport or the Chunnel's baggage checks, even with his police identification. He thought about Goh's contact in France, Lewis Smythe. The cop had told them that he could arrange anything they'd need in France.

They didn't have much more than a name to go on. Bolan wondered how much time he would have to devote to a search for Smythe. Then he'd have to arrange for tickets to France, storage of his war bag, and check on a few things that could be checked by the cybernetic warfare crew at Stony Man Farm.

If anything, the real problem was Tern and De Simmones. He was sure that they would be keeping watch for him at points of exit from London, and he knew that they would be fools to let him get to France without incident.

He pulled over and parked, reaching for his cell phone.

"Who are you calling?" Dean asked. Her voice was cold.

"Friends back home," Bolan answered. "I need some more intelligence on this, and to figure out who this Smythe guy is."

"Kevin trusts him." She thought about it a moment. "But then again, he trusted you too."

"Thanks for the vote of confidence."

Dean glared. "My sister, and now my partner. Have you ever worked with anyone whose life you didn't destroy?"

"Melissa, I'm sorry. I wish that—"

"It doesn't matter what you wish. Melanie is dead. Kevin's in a trauma ward. My career is going to be thrown in the shitter. And what the hell, we'll probably die fighting a team of heavily armed commandos."

"*We're* not going to die," Bolan stated. "You're staying in London."

Dean's eyes narrowed. "Fuck you. You do this damage… I nearly get killed twice tonight, and you want me to back off?"

"You're not obliged to risk your life."

"Did I mention you should piss off? Who appointed you the lone wolf?"

"I did. Going hunting for the people who hurt you only wrecks you to the core. I'm not someone doing this for a paycheck. I'm doing this because I died when my family was murdered years ago. I'm just taking one step at a time, doing everything I can to stop the suffering of others."

"You haven't done a good job today. I'm not backing off, this is personal now."

Bolan took a deep breath. "You do what I say. You follow my orders. If you screw up, you'll end up dead."

"And you're not worried about me doing something to get you killed?" Dean asked.

"Deliberately? No."

Dean suddenly lashed out, striking Bolan hard across his face. Her fist caught his nose and cheekbone, and his head recoiled. The pain stung, but he grimaced out a reflexive response. Dean swung her fist, catching Bolan stiffly on his jaw, turning his head.

"That's two. I'll give you three more," he told her in a low, raspy voice.

Dean paused.

"Go ahead! Get it out of your system. Throw everything at me that you can, but I'm only giving you for Melanie, Kevin, forcing you to kill and the two attempts on your life. Get it done, get the anger out. Then we can go on."

With a scream, the detective pummeled Bolan's head and face with three powerful punches. Dean's fourth punch was caught before it could land.

"I said, you get five for free."

As it was, Bolan could feel his left cheekbone swell, and blood trickled over his upper lip. His head hurt, and his lower lip burned where Dean had split it. She hit hard, and his brain still rattled with the rage of her blows.

"Feel better?" Bolan asked.

Dean shook her head. "And I don't think I would, even pounding you all day long."

"That's my point," Bolan said. "I fired shots to start the road that brought me here to London. They didn't take away an ounce of my pain. They only showed me that I had to be something different. That I had to fight for something other than petty anger."

Dean slumped back in the passenger seat for a moment. "I have my gun, you know."

"Never underestimate the power of dramatic effect."

"You were taking an awful big chance," Dean told him.

"I'm not the suicidal type. I knew you'd keep it under control." Bolan touched his tender and sore face. "At least mostly under control."

Bolan hit the dial button on his cell phone, linking him to Stony Man Farm.

WHEN BOLAN CALLED, the team at Stony Man Farm reacted instantly. He was not a man who worked on trivial matters, and even if he were only investigating the death of one person, as Hal Brognola had indicated earlier, things were lurking in the shadows of a larger, deadlier conspiracy.

Blowing away the mists that hid the lurkers in the darkness was the job of the cyberteam. Intelligence from satellites, computer databases and news sources provided the beacon with which they could direct Bolan, Able Team and Phoenix Force against these shadow dwellers, to find them and clear them out of the murky depths where they hid.

Aaron "The Bear" Kurtzman, Barbara Price and Hal Brognola were all present and on alert. The last few days of activity in London, including the Executioner's night-long blitz of the underworld, had put the Farm's core staff on maximum alert. Akira Tokaido, Carmen Delahunt and Huntington Wethers were all at their stations, working on their own projects, but ready to put them on hold at a moment's notice.

"Striker, we're online," Brognola spoke up. "Anything to report?"

"Keep an eye on Kevin Goh. He took some hits, and he's in the hospital. I want to keep updated on his condition," Bolan answered.

"We've got him covered," Price stated. "What's your plan?"

"I'm taking a trip to France. The Maginot Line."

"How?"

"Chunnel."

"Seems risky," Brognola said.

"Riskier to attempt a flight. The time spent at an airport renting a plane, or booking a proper flight to eastern France leaves us open for whoever Tern has at the airports looking for me."

"Tern?" Kurtzman asked.

"Liam Tern. And Etienne De Simmones. Both former SAS." Bolan read them the serial numbers for both men. "Back to the Chunnel, it's only twenty minutes across the Channel, and I'll have a car waiting on the other side."

"If you make it that far," Price said. "You said that Tern would have people at the airport. They'll sure as hell have people at the ferry and the Channel Tunnel."

"A stray shot at a train station won't bring down an airplane," Bolan told her. "Nothing to start an explosion."

"I've already got background data on Tern," Wethers said.

Delahunt spoke next. "De Simmones's operational history is heavy with rumors, but I'm tracking them down. He owns a small company in France—a security company with employees culled from the British army and the French armed forces, including the Foreign Legion."

"How legitimate is he?" Bolan asked.

"In terms of sheer money, $475 million in contracts for the past year," Delahunt answered.

"Is that mercenary money, or rent-a-cop money?" Bolan asked.

Kurtzman regarded Delahunt, her fingers working the keyboard, milking the search engine for all it could give her. She finally looked up.

"We're talking contracts in Africa and the Middle East. Saudi Arabia to be exact," Delahunt replied. "He's giving a prince some villa security way out in the middle of nowhere."

"And he has ownership of a satellite through a cutout," Tokaido interjected.

"Any data on the satellite?" Bolan asked.

"It passes over Europe on its regular orbit path. The ground control station is a microwave transmitter in eastern France. Small, relatively cheap, but the tranceiver is quite efficient."

"Bear, I need something else. A cop recommended this guy as a contact to me—Lewis Smythe. Said he'd be able to help me, but he's ex-Legion, like a couple of the people working for Tern and De Simmones."

Kurtzman got to work. "We'll have everything for you by the time you get to Paris. Do you still have your laptop?"

"I lost it in a confrontation with the enemy. I also lost the records for *The Clarion*. Its editor was murdered, and those drives could have given me a good idea who hired De Simmones to murder him."

"Carrington?" Kurtzman asked.

"Been keeping up on the mysterious deaths in my wake?" Bolan asked.

"You never know what would be a clue to helping you, Striker. Live large, big guy."

"You too," Bolan responded. He killed the connection.

IT WAS TIME TO MAKE another call.

"Hello again, Mr. Cooper," Tern said.

"You missed."

Tern didn't respond.

"You missed. And you lost your teammate. The machine gunner," Bolan said, taunting the madman. "I was dead center on target with him."

The Executioner was looking for a hot button. He hit it hard.

"You piece of shit. You think you can intimidate me?" Tern said, snapping.

"I'm sweeping your people up all across London. How

many more people in this country could Executive Action Enterprises have on either side of the law?" Bolan asked.

"So you know about Etienne—"

"And you, Liam."

It was a dead hit. Silence gripped the line for a moment. "You know nothing about me, American."

"I know you're enjoying this job. I know you've finally given in if you're the one in charge now. De Simmones is just sitting back, keeping himself safe, making no sudden movements to set you off. He's waiting for the chance to either ditch you or put two in your skull."

"The old man can try to kill me," Tern said, laughing.

"Just like you've tried to kill me? All I've got to show for your efforts is a pile of corpses, sprawled across the city. I've got a handle on you. And I intend to twist you until you break."

There was a grunt on the other end, then the sound of an impact. Bolan figured. Tern had thrown the cell phone across the room.

It was all part of the plan.

Tern was going to do his best to lure Bolan to him. The Executioner baited, and the killer's greed was going to get the better of him.

"Cooper!" he heard Tern call in the distance. Heavy foot treads sounded, coming toward the phone.

"Drop something?" Bolan asked him.

"You think you're funny."

"I'm dead serious."

"You're just dead," Tern snapped.

"I'll be seeing you, Liam."

Bolan hung up as he heard the growl rise on the other side. He'd done enough damage for the moment.

LIAM TERN LET THE PHONE drop to his feet. His eyes looked toward Etienne De Simmones. His lip curled, twitched up reflexively.

For a moment, the old man thought Tern was going to snap. He started to reach for his Walther but thought the better of it. A sudden movement would set Tern off.

"He's right," Tern said. He got it back under control, slicking back his hair, straightening his tie.

"What about?" De Simmones asked.

"You. You're just sitting back, afraid of making any sudden moves. You're watching me, waiting for me to snap, looking to get out of the way of any damage."

"Now hold on… He's trying to chip away at your resources. He's found a chink in your armor, and he's stabbing you through it. By the time he gets here—"

Tern shook his head. "You're scared, Etienne."

"Damn straight! You admitted to me that you're not right."

The knife snapped from Tern's sleeve, hitting his palm with a chilling slap.

"I'm pissed off, and I would love the opportunity to take out some frustration on someone. You're right here…" Tern reached up with his free hand, squeezing De Simmones's jowls together. "One snicker-snack, and all the red, red vino will come spilling down over your shirt, pretty as can be."

De Simmones was frozen, except for his throat. He swallowed hard, trying to get rid of the parched dryness that clogged it. He felt the scrape of metal on his skin and fought the urge to close his eyes. He wanted to face death.

"Etienne, you have a lot of control," Tern said with a smile.

The muscles in De Simmones's chest tightened as the spear tip of Tern's blade scratched gently down the front of his neck. No soft trickle of blood issued from the scrape, but he knew that could change with an ounce of pressure, a single reflexive flinch.

The blade glimmered again in De Simmones's peripheral vision. "You're too useful. I'm not going to kill you, even though you're right. He had me thinking about doing it."

"Thank you, Liam."

"Call me sir."

"Sir."

Tern smirked.

"Good work, old man." He gave De Simmones a light slap on the cheek and turned away. The veteran soldier thought about going for his gun and realized he felt lighter. The pressure of its steel frame was no longer tucked against his side. His heart sank.

"I'm not foolish enough to leave you with a means of killing me. You might not take me face to face, but you could catch me by surprise." Tern looked over his shoulder, a twinkle in his eye. "Though, I commend you for not patting yourself down, looking for this," he said, waving the Walther for De Simmones to see.

THE RAILEUROPE SECTION at Waterloo station was neat and orderly. Since the total turnaround time for the train's circuit was a mere forty minutes, it wasn't too crowded at that time of the morning. People commuting between England and France, with the proper passes bought at the counter, were lining up to get to Paris and points east.

Bolan requested access to an Internet terminal and was directed to one in the telephone kiosk. A dubiously secure device, the Executioner reassured himself that anything he got from the machine could be wiped clean by the experts at Stony Man Farm. He connected and keyed in to receive an e-mail from Kurtzman.

"'Once you get to Paris, we have a locker for you to a fresh laptop and replacement tools,'" the e-mail read.

Bolan memorized the information about the locker number he had to open. The key itself would be taped under the row of lockers in Paris's Gare du Nord station.

"Lewis Smythe is a man with a record of violent confrontations with American and French criminals. He was arrested once here but fled the country. The DEA has him on tap as a snitch overseas. He doesn't like heroin dealers but will scam anyone he can. Being in the French Foreign Legion kept him from being actively expedited for a few years until he arranged ties with the DEA."

Bolan was impressed with that bit of information. He studied Smythe's military record, which was contained in an attached text document. The man was a specialist in small-unit tactics, was an armorer and a sniper-scout. The last part meant not only was he a top marksman, but he was the kind of man who could sit and stake out an enemy forever, eyes never leaving his target. If anyone had the ability to gather information, it would be Smythe. Bolan memorized Smythe's address in Paris.

He looked at his watch. It was a quarter to five in the morning, and since 9/11, the trains between London and Paris had a full half-hour check-in time preceding boarding. Bolan made sure all of his gear, except for his two knives, were stashed in his war bag. Even Dean's pistols were hidden away in the nylon carry-all. He stowed them in a locker, then pocketed the key.

"Ready?" Bolan asked.

"As I'll ever be," Dean muttered.

Bolan was glad for her presence this far. Her badge and authority had allowed them to get on the train without prior reservations. Still, the little plastic identification card would only take them so far. They were going to be without any weapons except for the knives, and he'd surreptitiously handed her one. They would have to rely on their wits, their bodies and each other.

Not the ideal situation.

Almost three and a half hours before they got to Paris. And then on to Nancy, if they were going to continue by train to the nearest major RailEurope stop to Thionville.

It all depended on what went down when they met with Smythe.

Bolan felt the presence of the two shadows in the corner of his vision.

Tern's men. They were only watching. One was on the phone.

Neither man looked insane enough to have weapons in the well-guarded and patrolled Waterloo Station. But Bolan wasn't going to put it past them.

But he also realized that those same heavily armed guards weren't going to deter anyone from making an attempt once the three-hour journey was under way.

Bolan and Dean got in line. From her demeanor, he could see she was aware of their enemies too.

Whatever these men had in mind, it wouldn't be a surprise.

Not that it made Bolan's job of surviving any easier.

14

On the Chunnel trip, Bolan and Dean allowed themselves to relax in their passenger compartment. Built like an airliner, each individual car was a long, narrow tube with plush seats. Breakfast trays were delivered on meal carts by women who were beaming and polite despite the early hour.

Bolan cleaned his sunglasses, using the reflection to keep an eye on the two men shadowing them. He knew that Dean's badge had gotten them past the reservation requirements to get on the train. He wondered what Tern's men had used to get on the express train.

It was probably a lot of money spent. Bolan considered the ramifications that money could break the sanctity of the Chunnel's security measures. He knew that if someone wanted to, they could still get past any of the so-called anti-terrorism contingencies put in place by nations around the globe.

The blade in Bolan's pocket was proof that weapons could still be smuggled on board. Being made of titanium, not steel, it didn't register ferromagnetically. The same applied to his backup knife, given to Dean.

He considered that it could just as easily have been enough explosives to knock out an airplane window, or to damage a high-speed rail train's electrical system just as it accelerated past the point of no return.

The Executioner frowned as a worse thought struck him.

"What's wrong?" Dean asked.

"Thinking about work."

"Those two?" she continued.

"Yeah. They managed to slip past the reservation buffer. If they could do that, then De Simmones might have more pull than we thought. I'm going to have to push their hand before we get in the open, where they might be able to get a gun on us."

Dean nodded. "I'm ready for anything," she said. "I know you could get me killed playing your games."

"I'm sorry about Kevin—"

"And I don't mean to accuse you of getting Kevin shot."

Bolan nodded. "Regardless, you two got involved with me because I stumbled onto the Ripper murder. Your case. I turned it over and made it into this war."

"Sure. And if you hadn't, we'd either be looking for clues in all the wrong places, or the Ripper and his pals would have come after us anyway. A squad of commando-trained murdering thugs against two unsuspecting, unarmed cops." Dean smiled. "We're probably a lot better off than we could have been."

Bolan shrugged. "It's nice to see someone who can look on the bright side of things."

He glanced back, catching the pair of De Simmones's men in his peripheral vision. He knew there was no advantage to be gained in feigning ignorance to their existence. Maybe by letting them know he knew where they were, he could spook them into a mistake.

AT CALAIS, THE TRAIN switched tracks and continued south toward Paris. It was a short break, but the train was soon rocketing at full speed along toward its destination. Bolan excused himself and made his way down the aisle toward the back of the railcar.

De Simmones's men watched him and Bolan stared, eyes

hard and glaring, never wavering from the two of them as he made his approach. The cold, icy gaze was the same he used when he interrogated suspects. One of the men shifted uncomfortably in his seat.

Bolan lifted his hand from his pocket swiftly and pointed a finger at them, as if he were drawing the Desert Eagle. They started in their seats.

"You look a little jumpy, lads," the Executioner whispered to them, before heading to the washroom to splash some cold water his face.

He took his time. He wanted to gauge their reaction. Knuckles rapped at the door as soon as he finished drying his hands with the vent. Bolan reached for the door slowly, giving himself some space in case it was his friends.

The door swung open. It was one of them, glaring at him. He held a pen in one hand, gripped like an ice pick.

The Executioner had seen enough poison injectors disguised as pens to figure out that he had less than a heartbeat to act.

The two men reacted in the same instant.

The killer with the poison pen jabbed, trying to slash and strike Bolan as he leaned back onto the sink and brought his steel toe up into the shin of his attacker.

Bolan kicked again, taking the other man's knee and knocking him back with a strained grunt of pain.

The killer looked down the aisle of the train car. People were turning, looking back at the ruckus. The element of surprise was blown, and now, engaged in a full-on conflict, the killer was going to have to finish the job or find a way to flee.

Since the train was rumbling along at close to 200 miles per hour, and the junctures between the cars were sealed, escape wasn't an option. The poison-armed killer raised his lethal stinger and lunged again. Bolan intercepted his forearm with a quick grab, then twisted his body. The two men slipped past each other in the tiny space of the bathroom, before the powerful arms of the Executioner rammed the smaller attacker's head into the bathroom mirror.

It was made of unbreakable stainless steel, and the only marring of the surface came from blood splashing from split skin. The thug kicked and twisted to escape Bolan, but the soldier held on tight to the man's wrist, wrenching with all of his might. The killer shrieked in pain.

The Executioner lashed out with a palm to the nose of the attacker, breaking it and smashing the man's front teeth. With a surge, he hurled his opponent to the floor, but the fight was already out of him. De Simmones's man lay like a puddle after a storm.

Bolan took his knife out and dropped it to the floor next to the unconscious man, then bent over and scooped up the pen.

The stewards rushed up, faces wide with shock, but Bolan had his badge out.

"This man came at me with a knife," Bolan said. He hoped that enough of the battle had occurred out of sight of the passengers to make the story believable. He didn't want to have wasted his knife in a useless excuse if they didn't buy it.

De Simmones's other man rose and grabbed a nearby child.

"We're all going to be calm, all right?" he said. A knife glimmered in his hand, its point pressed against the neck of the little boy, who was sobbing. "Anyone fucks with me, this little brat's going to die."

"We don't want that," Bolan told him. "Just be cool."

The thug smirked. "You... I want what you took from my buddy."

"What are you talking about?" Bolan asked.

"I told you not to fuck with me," the knife man growled. "I'll saw this little prick's head off and piss down his neck if you mess with me!"

The child was screaming. If Bolan had been armed, this would have been over in a heartbeat, one .44 Magnum slug right at the bridge of the nose destroying the killer's brain before he could even react.

Bolan drew the pen.

"Give it over," the panicky thug said.

"Okay."

Bolan took a step forward, holding it out toward the knife man.

"Give it to the kid," the nervous man said. He gave his hostage a squeeze for emphasis. Bolan was disgusted by the cowardly display.

The boy reached up. His eyes met Bolan's.

The Executioner gave him a nod and held the pen above his hand. "And when you get the pen?"

"I still hold on to the brat. He's my ticket off this train."

The Executioner gave the pen a click. The nib poked out the end.

"There's no call for that."

The goon was extremely nervous, pulling away from Bolan. He was backing toward Dean, apparently having forgotten about her in all the excitement.

Bolan maintained his command of the situation. He stepped forward, holding out the pen, gently, loosely. The lethal point was aimed at the man's heart.

"You're so hot to have the pen...."

"Back off or the kid's head comes off."

"You'd think this pen was dangerous," Bolan said.

"I'll cut this kid's throat out," De Simmones's man threatened.

With a sudden lunge, Dean plowed into the killer's back.

Bolan surged forward, hands locked on the forearm that pressed the knife to the boy's throat. In a mad frenzy, the quartet of bodies whirled in the aisle.

The knife point scratched across Bolan's stomach, his shirt parted and blood flowed, drawn by the gleaming point. Bolan used a head butt, his skull smashing into the man's nose. At the same time, the Executioner turned. Leverage forced the renegade's knife arm up, and his elbow snapped to full extension. With a hard punch into the man's shoulder, the elbow joint popped.

On the other side of the conflict, Dean wasn't sitting still. Her fists pummeled the thug's kidneys.

The knife dropped to the floor, bounced once and was out of consideration for the rest of the fight.

The boy squirmed loose and ran back to safety.

Bolan punched the thug under his ribs, releasing a spray of blood as the breath was blown out of him, powering through the gory fountain of the man's wrecked features. Bolan ignored the mess and rammed a left just behind the man's jaw, striking him on the neck, where blood vessels and nerves were at their most vulnerable. The blow was an instant knockout, and the soldier lowered the killer to the ground.

Dean looked at Bolan. "What now?"

"Those were the only two that I know were on this train," Bolan replied. "We should be okay for the rest of the train ride."

"What's going on?" a steward asked.

Bolan flashed his badge again. "We were heading to France on a joint investigation. She's Scotland Yard. I'm Boston PD."

"This man, and the man who attacked Cooper in the bathroom, they're part of a conspiracy to commit murder," Dean said.

"Do you have any cable ties?" Bolan asked.

"For garbage bags?" the steward asked.

Bolan nodded. The woman spoke swiftly to another of the attendants. Cable ties were brought quickly, and the unconscious thugs were restrained.

Bolan got on the phone to Stony Man Farm.

He was going to need more of Hal Brognola's diplomatic magic to keep them from being bogged down by the Paris gendarmes.

He had a meeting with Lewis Smythe, and he didn't want to get caught by the enemy without a gun.

LIAM TERN STRETCHED OUT and regarded the office around him. De Simmones had done a good job with their headquarters. Instead of a hole in a mountainside where space was at a minimum, the SAS man managed to secure them in an area that was built up during the fifties and sixties for French government to hide under hundreds of feet of stone if nuclear missiles started falling.

The place was designed for the government to hole up for months, even years, so comfort was as much of a necessity as supplies, communications and resistance to a point-blank atomic blast. The office Tern claimed had been furnished over forty years earlier and was adorned with classically designed furniture. It was nothing like the stale, colorless, unstyled monotony of the cubicle farms just down the hall. Though there was no sunlight this far down, there were lights and mirrors that gave the illusion of warmth and daytime.

Tern passed in front of the full-length mirror again and made sure that the four Berettas were snug under his jacket, well hidden away.

He'd like to meet Cooper and end this fight with him with the feel of a knife in flesh. It would be most satisfying to feel the resistance of muscle and tough organ fibers against the blade as hot blood washed over his hand. Tern smiled, feeling excitement tingle throughout his body. His heart rate escalated as he thought about Cooper squirming and dying as they were connected by six deadly inches of steel.

Tern closed his eyes, dismissing the thought. Cooper was too good. Giving in to the pleasure of the kill was too risky. Fighting an opponent equal to his own abilities would require distance and cool reserve.

It would be better to pull his pistols and drop a 9 mm slug into the man who was treading on his hopes and dreams.

He would make sure Cooper was dying, and if there was enough of him left when he was on his back, unable to lift his hands to defend himself, then he could ram his knife between the man's ribs. Tern grinned.

"Thinking happy thoughts?"

Tern whirled.

"He's not here yet," De Simmones said, answering Tern's unspoken question. "He came through the Chunnel, but I'm already hearing reports about two men being arrested for assault on the train."

"Arrested?" Tern asked.

"If they'd been allowed to take their guns with them I doubt it would have gone so well," De Simmones stated. "Cooper and his companion are exposing too much of my operation. And when they're putting that much light on me, that means we're getting scrutiny from the governments we're working for."

"So?"

"Even if we take care of Cooper, we have lost the element of anonymity. I'm pretty much a dead man."

Tern frowned.

"I didn't think you were that concerned with my life," De Simmones said.

"I'm not really, not if you're trying to fuck me over, but if we're talking about having others come after us, then new plans have to be made."

Tern walked back to the desk and leaned against it, looking down. "Do they know where you've set up shop?"

"Yeah. We'll have to lose the tunnels as a headquarters. There'll also be legal measures against Executive Action Systems."

"How much of our money is tied up with them?" Tern asked.

"Not much, but enough to give me a shot in the wallet."

"Could we set up elsewhere?"

"With the money I do have? Yeah. Everything's in secure bank accounts."

Tern nodded. "You have the beginnings of a back door for us?"

"I'm insulted that you have to ask me," De Simmones replied.

Tern smiled. "How long do you think they'll give us?"

"Days. If that."

"I figured as much. But I'd rather worry about one threat at a time, not two."

"And Cooper?"

"We have men at the Gare du Nord?" Tern asked, referring to the rail hub in Paris.

"Three. Armed."

"Are you willing to lose them?" Tern asked

"We've lost so many, what's three more? You think Cooper can somehow miraculously defeat three armed men without his weapons?" De Simmones asked.

"He defeated five in a hospital starting with nothing more than a bedpan," Tern said. "Cooper is a fighting man. He's not some gunslinger. To him, survival is something that runs through every fiber of his being. You throw him against a wall, and he'll bounce back in your face. He's not a man to be trifled with."

"I know the type. That kind of man is rare," De Simmones replied. "I would have loved to get him in my unit back in the day. We'd have torn down anyone we went against. But right now, I have three men with automatic weapons at a train station full of armed cops."

"Your point?" Tern asked.

"They'll be throwaways. I'm calling them back here. We're going to make a concentrated defense on home turf. If you want to wear him down some more, then we'll meet him in town. He'll have to pass through Thionville. And knowing someone like him, he'll pay a visit to our offices."

Tern smirked.

"You have an idea?" De Simmones asked.

"A killer plan. It might even work against this guy. But even if it doesn't, we'll do a little house cleaning. Make Her Majesty and the French think that Cooper has taken care of us, once and for all."

De Simmones smiled. "Yeah. I get what you're thinking."

"It all comes down to seeing if Matt Cooper can survive in a building that's blowing itself to hell."

"And the men we lose will naturally confuse the body count. Why, the two of us could be among the dead."

"We'll tell our boys to get a couple of men matching our descriptions, and then we can switch dental records. By the time anyone figures out we're not among the dead—"

De Simmones threw his arms wide open. "You and I will be sitting on a beach, sipping margaritas. If they ever figure it out at all."

Tern chuckled. "Let's not get too cocky."

"You're right. What about the girls?"

"We'll leave them down here. Why waste the ammunition? They'll just starve to death. Even worse, they'll dehydrate. Three, five days, and it's over for them."

"You're a cold man."

Tern shrugged. "What did you expect? I'd go and do the job myself? There's no fun in killing a caged animal."

15

Bolan and Dean gave their statements to the gendarmerie about the incident with the two would-be murderers on the train from London. Brognola's diplomatic skills insured that they didn't have to go through long, detailed interviews over the use of force on De Simmones's hit men. The only request was that Bolan and Dean would be available for further interviews when it came time to prosecute the attackers.

The Executioner would never return for such trivialities. He had a final knockout blow to deliver, and sticking around for the bureaucratic process wasn't anywhere on his agenda.

Bolan took half an hour to make sure that they weren't being followed after getting off at the Gare du Nord and completing their statements to the police. To some small surprise, there was nobody trailing them. Bolan gave an extra ten minutes to double-check for any tails after renting a car, then he and Dean went to pay a visit to Lewis Smythe.

After a day of throwing manpower at him, Tern and De Simmones seemed to have clued-in that more thugs wasn't the answer. Bolan knew they were mobbing up, probably at Thionville, and definitely at the Immerhoff hardsite.

That meant things were going to be that much more difficult. The two masterminds of the Ripper operation were thinking, not panicking, not wasting their dwindling resources. The Executioner didn't know how much he had left to fight through, but he recalled the machine gunner's statement of heavily trained, well-armed men waiting to greet him.

He hoped Goh's friend, Smythe, would have good guns and gear.

Smythe was easy enough to find. He had a small office in a building that had little else in it. Bolan suspected that Smythe probably owned the whole building. Dean was grimly silent as they moved up the stairs, ignoring the elevator that would take them to the third floor. There was only one door on the landing besides the exit from the elevator cage, and it was the listing for Smythe.

Bolan rapped his knuckles on the door. It opened and he came face-to-face with a tall, bald black man who looked him over for a moment. Lean, with no wasted mass, and long, slender arms and legs wrapped in the fine black silk of a suit, he had a regal visage that was marred by the single line of fused flesh that ran from his eyebrow through one eye to the corner of his mouth. Both eyes were clear, however, paying close attention to the two people who entered his office. Whatever had caused the injury to his face had spared his eye.

"My name's Cooper. This is Melissa Dean. We're friends of Kevin Goh," Bolan said.

"Your not name's not Cooper, but that doesn't matter. Come in," Smythe answered. He stepped to one side, letting them both enter. The office was neatly kept, almost empty, except for a desk with a telephone and a computer.

"Doing research?" Bolan asked.

"Goh called me. He woke up an hour ago and phoned ahead to let me know I'd have a couple of visitors."

Bolan studied his face. It was an inscrutable mask.

"Kevin gave me the lowdown on you, Cooper. You're no cop."

Bolan shrugged.

"Figured as much. Melissa, nice to finally meet you," Smythe stated.

"Kevin's talked about me?" Dean asked.

"Said that you're the best partner he's ever had."

Dean smiled and tried to hide a blush.

"Okay, Kevin said you two were looking to do some carnage out by the Maginot Line. A town called Thionville."

"Know the place?" Bolan asked.

"Not personally. But I did some research."

Bolan read the results off the printer. Some of it was research from the Boston Police Department records. He saw the Matt Cooper identity staring him in the face, red circles and red crosses skewering bits and pieces of the data they had on him. Stony Man Farm had built him a good cover identity, but apparently it hadn't flown with the tall ex-legionnaire.

"Kevin only called you an hour ago?" Bolan asked, surprised with what Smythe had learned so quickly.

"I know a few things about search engines," Smythe answered. "I've been paying attention to the news out of London. CNN is all over the sudden explosion in gang wars. First Sonny Westerbridge goes splat, then the rest of the organizations start detonating. Things are getting back under control, people are getting sane again this morning, but it was still pretty unique," Smythe responded.

Bolan simply nodded.

Smythe got to the point. "You'll be needing weapons and gear. Would you like some backup?"

"What kind could I get?" Bolan asked.

"Me."

"Nothing else?"

"I have a pilot. But he doesn't have commando training. He can get us from Paris to Thionville, which is a step over from Immerhoff."

"Why not Immerhoff itself?" Dean asked.

"Immerhoff is just a fort. Thionville is an actual town, with a couple of major highways and rail lines running to it," Bolan and Smythe spoke simultaneously.

"Sorry," Smythe said.

"It's okay. I guess they're right about great minds."

Smythe smiled. "I'm not sure what else you'd like. Kevin stated that you had a Desert Eagle and some kind of silenced Beretta as part of your gear."

Smythe lead them up the stairs to another suite of nearly empty offices. He went to one desk and slid its top off, revealing a display of handguns in red velvet cutouts. He reached down and picked up a huge, familiar-looking handgun.

"I don't usually go for the Desert Eagle, and as such, don't have any in my personal reserve. They sell fast among mercenaries wanting to ship to Africa. You can guess that at least they'd like to be able to put a .44 Magnum slug into an elephant if the morons can ever find one," Smythe explained.

Bolan nodded. "What is that thing?"

Smythe handed the pistol over and Bolan felt the almost familiar weight in the palm of his hand. "A Wildey Survivor. In .44 Automag. One of my personal favorites."

The long, sleek lines of the handgun balanced well in Bolan's hand. The gun felt like an extension of his body.

The Executioner suppressed a smile in reminiscence of his old friend Big Thunder. "I think I can make do with this. Any place where I can sight in?" he asked.

"I've got a range in the basement," Smythe replied. He took one for himself, and a bunch of magazines. "Anything else you're looking for?"

"I'd say Dean should use a Glock or Beretta, whichever of those you have ready for use," Bolan said.

"How about if I pick?" Dean asked, indignant. "You do a lot of bossing, and now you're presuming?"

"Perhaps I can let you two discuss this among yourselves," Smythe interjected.

Dean glared.

"I'm sorry. I don't want to argue with you, but if you feel like fighting, I suggest you save it for Tern and De Simmones," Bolan said.

"Fine," Dean answered. "But you're still on my shit list. We'll go with the Glocks. The Beretta felt too fat in my hand. And if you're going to carry something with real punch, I want a gun with kick too."

"Got anything in mind?" Bolan asked.

"Glock 21 in 10 mm, if you have one, Mr. Smythe," Dean requested. "And for the silenced Glocks, let's go with the Glock 19 if you have them. That way the magazines are designed differently and we can't confuse them."

"Good thinking," Smythe replied. "What about long arms?"

"What's the best of what you have left?" Bolan asked. "I'm sure you can hardly keep MP-5s in stock."

"We're not going to be doing a lot of outdoor shooting, are we?" Smythe asked. "I'm anticipating close quarters work."

"Under the Maginot Line, and maybe in town. But I'd still like a little punch and a lot of accuracy," Bolan said.

Smythe led him to a wall display. Removing a couple paintings, the arms dealer revealed a wall full of mounted machine guns flush with the plaster.

"The 48. About the length of your standard American squad-car-issued shotgun, but with all the punch and power of an M-60 light machine gun," Smythe said. "I kept one or two for my personal work. I love it."

Bolan took it down. "Nice."

"It's not a personal minigun, but it is very nice," Smythe returned. "It can lay down 710 rounds per minute in full-auto, but is as controllable as a rifle. There are accommodations for all NATO standard optics."

"I want something with a little more portability. Do you have any Olympic Arms OA-93 machine pistols?" Bolan asked.

Smythe nodded. "A man who knows what he needs. I'll bring the M-48 along with us, but the OA-93s are a good choice. Silencers, though, are a must."

"Why?" Dean asked.

"The muzzle-blast, in an enclosed space like a tunnel or a building, will turn your brains to pudding if you're not protected. Hearing protectors would be a good idea too."

"And we'll need clothing. Proper clothing, especially for Dean," Bolan said.

The cop looked down at herself, then at Bolan. She remembered the skintight blacksuit he'd worn the night before while he was delivering mayhem to the underworld of London. "Yeah. Something like that body stocking?"

"I've got an idea what you're both talking about," Smythe said.

"Smythe," Dean spoke up, "you don't sell all this good stuff to mercenaries, do you?"

"Nope. I sell them AK-47s and used, Vietnam-era M-16s," Smythe replied. "These are for my special purposes."

Dean raised an eyebrow.

"Let's just say I have my own vendetta against thugs who deal heroin in this city," Smythe replied. "This is just a favor to my buddy Kevin."

Bolan nodded. "Thank you."

Smythe nodded. "Thank you. Last night, you did what I've been wanting to do for a long time."

MELISSA DEAN DIDN'T MIND the waiting anymore. She was on a plane, headed somewhere. The tedious busywork of sighting in weapons, strapping gear into bags, making sure uniforms fit snugly, everything gave her mind focus.

She was calm, and that concerned her. She looked at the bag at her feet, full of ugly lumps of plastic, steel and gunpowder. Cooper had made sure that she knew how to handle everything. Nothing would be out of control for her. Though the machine pistol jumped a lot, she learned to lean into it and use her weight to tame its kick.

She even dropped the idea of the 10 mm Glock when she tried out the Wildey. Her long fingers were able to grasp the gun, and her upper-body strength was enough, when combined with the weight of the pistol, to fire it quickly and accurately in rapid fire. She could put seven shots in a space the size of a grapefruit in four seconds.

"It can be tough your first time," Bolan said.

"What can?" Dean asked.

"The ride. I've been watching your face the whole time. If you need to talk—"

"I'm fine," she said.

"Good," Bolan said.

"What's going on on the screen?" Dean asked.

Bolan showed her the screen on the borrowed laptop. Hooked to Bolan's phone, the little computer unit was in touch with Stony Man Farm over encrypted data links. There were maps popping up next to newspaper articles.

"We've got a time line from those articles you listed. I was right about the woman being used as a distraction for another assassination. All the instances of a Ripper murder to date have coincided with the death or disappearance of either investigative reporters or government fact finders."

"Someone's been using a series of serial murders to sweep other secrets under the carpet," Dean said.

"I've seen enough of these kinds of things to realize that the men in charge don't care about normal people," Bolan said. "Murdering a family doesn't mean a thing to these guys if they think you're between them and their cause."

"So we stop them?"

"Cold dead."

"Do we have a plan?"

"I have people researching the new construction for the facility where Tern and De Simmones have set up. So far, the maps are inconclusive, and there's no telling what's being used and where exactly. Apparently there's also natural geographical formations that could have made things easier for them to expand even more. It's enough to hide an army," Bolan said.

"So how are we going to get any advantage down in those depths?" Smythe called from the front.

"Thionville is where Etienne De Simmones has an office for Executive Action Enterprises," Bolan answered.

"De Simmones wouldn't keep much of an army in town. Mostly just office staff," Smythe said.

"It depends on how much he feels like throwing at me on site."

Dean thought about it. "It'll be a trap."

"That's why I'm going inside alone."

IT WAS NIGHT when the Executioner arrived at Thionville, a town of roughly forty thousand people with a well-developed industrial and office district.

The office building stood three stories tall, and Executive Action Enterprises was the only occupant. Bolan was certain that at night, the place would be devoid of almost any nonessential staff. Mobbing up in preparation for the Executioner's assault, the SAS vets would pull out anyone who'd get in the way, leaving behind only hardened fighting machines.

If he was lucky.

He left Smythe and Dean to perform their part of the plan, circling the building on two circuits. He familiarized himself with the architecture of the building, then slipped close, pausing at a Dumpster not far from the back door. He shed his overcoat and unveiled his skintight bodysuit. A Kevlar vest with pouches for spare ammunition and other gear covered his chest. He removed a tin of black greasepaint and coated his cheeks, chin and forehead, before going to work on his hands. Finally, he withdrew the sound-suppressed OA-93 machine pistol from its bag. He was ready for battle.

The back door was guarded by two men, each holding a sawed-off shotgun. Stepping out into the open, he caught the attention of one of the sentries, who squinted, having difficulty making out the shadowy form in the darkness. The guard raised his gun and took aim.

Bolan tapped the trigger on the machine pistol, and 5.56 mm NATO slugs tore into the gunner's chest and belly, disemboweling him instantly. The second gunman whirled and brought up his shotgun, but the Executioner had only to shift his aim a few degrees. A second salvo of autofire silenced the shotgunner before he could react.

Bolan had his advantage so far. No bullets had hit the door to alert any guards inside. He reached the door and checked it. It wasn't locked, and he slipped in. The halls were dimly lit, but he still stood out, absolute zero against shades of gray. That was how he wanted it, the psychological effect of a midnight hunter, a living shadow, terrorizing his enemies.

He lowered the OA-93 and padded down the hall, then pulled to a halt when a lone figure passed into view. The sentinel was smoking a pungent cigarette, a Walther P99 in his other hand.

Bolan slipped behind the guy man after checking to be sure that he wasn't with anyone else, then snaked his arm around the man's neck. With a sudden jerk, the Executioner had the guard in a chokehold, thumb jammed hard against the base of the man's skull. A few instants of pressure and the man's legs gave out, unconsciousness taking him.

Bolan needed someone to interrogate. He dragged the man behind a receptionist's desk in the lobby, securing his arms and legs with cable ties, then stuffing the man's own handkerchief in his mouth. Duct tape completed the gag.

He headed for the stairs.

DEAN FOUND a suspicious-looking man sitting in a Fiat, watching the EAE offices. If he'd heard anything, or seen anything of Cooper entering the building, there was no clue. There was no cue from the big American that he was going inside, or where he was at that moment.

All she knew was that there would possibly be someone outside, getting ready to slam the door shut on a very lethal trap.

She gave a nod to Smythe, who was down the sidewalk. He gave her a thumbs-up for her to act. She nodded again and walked up to the car. If this was just an innocent man sitting in his car on a week night, then she'd feel embarrassed. But there was something about him, something that set off her investigator's instincts.

It seemed like he was primed, sitting like a hunter waiting for his prey to come along.

His window was rolled down keeping his windshield from fogging up in the cold, and he was bundled in a warm jacket and wool hat. She noticed this much as she came up on him, then hauled out the Wildey Survivor and pressed the vented five-inch barrel against his cheek.

"Wake up and tell me why you're sitting here, or so help me, your head's going across the street," she said.

The man froze. "Wait!"

He spoke English as if he was just off the streets of London.

"Hands on the steering wheel. Any funny moves, and we'll both get to see what a .44 Automag does to a bloke's cabbage," Dean snapped.

He lifted a small box in his hand. "I don't have a gun. Just this."

"Toss it out here."

"It's my life insurance, bitch. It's called a dead-man trigger."

"Smythe! Tell Matt to get the hell out!" she shouted.

Dean stepped back, keeping the front sight of the Wildey aimed at the man's head.

"I'm leaving now, bitch." He reached for the ignition, the engine turning over. The car slipped into gear.

She triggered a round toward the dashboard. The center of the steering wheel exploded, an airbag burst into life and inflated in the driver's face.

Across the street, a window shattered, and seconds later, a concussion wave swept over her.

The Fiat screeched away from the curb, careening out of control into a traffic light.

The driver stumbled out, snarling and cursing, bringing up a handgun when Smythe, long, lean, black and mean in his trench coat, stepped from the shadows and opened fire. De Simmones's man staggered as two .44 Automag hollowpoint rounds tore through his body, folding him over.

"Check on Cooper!" Smythe yelled.

Dean's head was ringing from the shock wave she'd been through, then she looked across the street. Flames belched out the second floor windows all around the office building, and on the sidewalk, a man was struggling to all fours. It was Bolan and she ran over to him, but he waved her off.

"It was a trap…" he confirmed. "Thankfully, that hogleg you decided to carry was loud enough for me to hear from inside."

"You jumped out the window?"

Bolan nodded. He looked himself over and didn't find any apparent wounds.

The building shook again as secondary explosions erupted inside. He turned back, remembering the unconscious smoker he'd left in the lobby.

Smythe's rented car screeched to a halt.

"We have to go! Police scanner is picking up the local cops. They'll be here any minute."

"Give me a minute!" Bolan yelled, already running.

He plunged into the lobby of the burning building, but was cut short as part of the ceiling came down. Chunks slammed into the desk that he'd hidden the man behind. A blast of flame rolled down the steps and over the niche where he'd tucked the body.

"Cooper!" Dean called.

The bombs explained everything. EAE had become expendable. Bolan had discovered two corpses, their bodies sprawled across a desk, stitched with bullet holes. De Simmones and Tern were using him as an excuse to clean house and disappear.

The Executioner turned and raced to Smythe's car.

From hell came the original Jack the Ripper.

Back to hell Tern and his master would go.

16

As late as the mid-1960s, the fortress of Immerhoff, along the Maginot Line, was a NATO radio communications station. That much was public knowledge. Immerhoff's entrance poked from a hillside, the facade of the building grown over with lush green grass that seemed almost inviting, even at night.

The illusion was that this place was long abandoned, the memory of a folly forgotten from World War II.

The Executioner knew better. The Maginot Line was a success. Thousands of German soldiers died while trying to penetrate it along various segments. The heavy guns and the vigilant French defenders held their ground, repelling the Nazi attackers. Only by slipping past the line's limits did the German forces manage to get a foothold into France.

Bolan had invaded a lot of places called fortresses before. This was literally a fort. Yet, for all its masonry and steel, the men who had it under their control were seeking to use the protection of privacy and secrecy.

Smythe unlimbered the M48 and hung a canvas-wrapped box of belted 7.62 mm NATO rounds on the side, closing the bolt over a live round. He double-checked a Reed Knight sound suppressor built for the light machine gun, then gave Bolan a thumbs-up. Dean prepped her Olympic Arms machine pistol the same way she'd watched Bolan prepare his. She gave a subtle nod to inform him that she was ready.

"Let's do it. Be careful," Bolan said.

The three of them bypassed the entrance.

Instead, they found the ventilation hatch-emergency exit that Aaron Kurtzman discovered had been built as part of the NATO new construction, but wasn't on the continuity of government building records.

It was risky. Tern would likely have men covering it if he knew about it, but there was no choice.

Going in the front door would be suicide. However, getting caught in a tunnel on a ladder, with two bodies above him, would also prove to have its risks. The Executioner looked at his two companions and shook his head. He pointed to himself, then down the hole. He handed a pair of flash-bang grenades to them and shimmied down the ladder.

Bolan was taking a gamble, but that was an everyday part of his life. If he encountered anyone at the bottom of the shaft, then he'd make enough racket for the other two to drop their stun grenades down the hole.

He started down the rungs.

Somewhere, down in the darkness, death waited for the Executioner to make his final play in the battle against the Ripper.

"GET THE MEN ON ALERT," De Simmones said, coming in from the communications center. "The offices in town were blown."

Tern smirked. "How long ago?"

"Half hour, forty-five minutes. Reports are inconclusive," the old vet stated. "Cooper's on his way here—"

"Or he's already on his way down," Tern stated. He pulled his cloak from the coatrack and swung it around his shoulders. With a flourish, he flipped the disguise's top hat onto his head.

"What are you doing?" De Simmones asked.

"Getting into the part, Etienne."

De Simmones stared.

"Cooper came to battle the Ripper. Well I'm giving him that much."

The older renegade shook his head. "Unbelievable."

"So's a single man ripping apart an organization of SAS trained gunmen."

Tern stepped into the hall, his cape swelling with his movement. He paused, and the cloak collapsed against his back. He unbuttoned his suit coat, and the clack of the holstered Berettas sounded in the veterans' ears.

"Are you armed?" Tern asked.

"No. You took my Walther."

Tern faced De Simmones and flipped him the small pocket pistol. "Go get yourself an HK. Mr. Cooper just set off the intruder alarm."

Tern lowered his head, smiling. The rush hit his veins, which he imagined had to be the same sort of surge that a junkie felt when the smack hit their bloodstream.

It was showtime.

THE EXECUTIONER DROPPED the last six feet, landing in a crouch, Glock out and probing the door at the bottom. He gave it a test and saw the red blip of a pressure sensor suddenly go off. With a curse, Bolan twisted the handle and pulled open the hatch. There were no men visible on the other side, he could hear the thunder of racing feet before he saw the shades that rushed to meet him.

Bolan extended his Glock 19 in one fist, his other hand gripping the handle of the OA-93.

One of the defenders of the underground tunnel stopped to shoulder a machine pistol, but Bolan cut him off with a 9 mm pill from the Glock. The gunner jerked as the back of his head exploded in a cone of chunky brains and blood.

Bolan dropped to his side to land on his thigh. Bullets sliced the air above him. The Executioner extended both weapons in his fists, as triggers worked to pump out bullets one at a time. It was sloppy shooting, but Bolan watched two more men stumble and fall flat on their faces, never to rise again as his salvo of return fire cut through them. Another gunman retreated to the cover of a support beam. He screamed as blood poured out from his guts.

Bolan rolled as the last gunman in the hall adjusted his aim. He felt the sting of flying concrete splinters lash at his back, but he came out laying prone, the Olympic Arms machine pistol lifted sideways from the ground to keep its magazine from barking on the floor. Bolan pulled the trigger twice and caught the final sentry in the belly. The guard twisted in agony, and Bolan followed up with a mercy round from the Glock, smashing open the dying man's skull.

No one else rushed to engage the Executioner, and he looked back to the hatch. Dean was down first, her machine pistol leading the way. She stepped into the hall before the mass of Smythe fell to the floor behind her.

"I thought I told you to drop those flash-bangs in case I was in the middle of some trouble," Bolan said.

"We were going to, but the shooting stopped too quickly," Dean answered.

She lifted her OA-93 and aimed at the man who cowered behind cover down the hall. Dean lowered her gun when she saw that he was busy controlling his blood loss.

"The lights don't extend much farther that way," Smythe said.

No sooner had he spoken those words when the tunnels were plunged into complete darkness. Dean cursed and clicked on a flashlight.

Bolan shoved her hard and dived to the floor, bullets buzzing through the air like furious yellow jackets. Dean quickly killed her light.

"Damn," she said.

"Sorry," Bolan answered.

"Don't be sorry for that one. I was the one who made myself a neon target—"

"Hang back here. Smythe, get ready to make some noise," Bolan whispered.

He nestled against the wall, where he felt the swell of a support brace jut out to protect his body. Curling his legs behind the protection of the outcropping, he withdrew a light stick and cracked it open. The green haze spilled out, and he was pleased to see that Smythe and Dean were using the hatchway for cover. He reached into his harness for something he anticipated would be useful for fighting in subterranean tunnels.

The steel U with an elastic band was a simple tool, a toy from before he was even born. But the slingshot also had practical utility. Especially for what he had in mind. Cupping the light stick in the centering pouch of the elastic number, Bolan cocked back the device, leaned out and fired down the hall in one smooth movement. He rolled forward, tucking tight as gunfire sliced the air where he'd been only moments before.

The green, glowing rod skittered down the hall, and after a moment came to a rest at the feet of the gunmen. They looked down at the little illuminating packet of chemicals, then up the tunnel, in confusion.

Smythe swung around, the M48 erupting. Even though the weapon had a sound suppressor, it was loud and thumping, the air shaking as each high velocity 7.62 mm slug ripped through the air in the closed-in tunnels. With rounds pounding them at 710 per minute, the Ripper's men danced, their bodies perforated with dozens of new openings. Bolan brought his OA-93 to bear, batting cleanup to catch anyone the bald man's machine gun missed. Within instants, the hallway was twice as littered with corpses as it had been before.

A couple of moans and wails from injured men filled the air, and the Executioner took point past them. As he passed, he saw only one man claw his way up the wall to fight. Bolan put a Glock bullet through his head and let him slide back to rest in peace. No one else was alive or conscious to give them any further resistance.

Smythe walked parallel to Bolan, Dean bringing up the rear.

"We're too bunched up," Bolan said. He scanned ahead. The shadows promised only more carnage. Already the tunnels stunk with the coppery reek of spilled blood.

"We'll hopscotch," Smythe said. "Or I should be on point."

He patted the side of the machine gun in his hands.

"I prefer the hopscotch. I can't ask anyone to go where I wouldn't go first," Bolan answered.

"I figured you were that kind of man," Smythe replied. "I'll light up the tunnel from here. You go."

Smythe activated the Sure-Fire gun light clipped to his weapon's barrel, a cone of brilliant blue illumination slashing through the blackness. He caught a figure jerk out of the way in an instant, and was about to tap the trigger when Dean's weapon snarled. Bullets tore into a filing cabinet's frame making aluminum pop. A strangled cry issued forth, and the body toppled back through their line of sight, Dean following up her first burst with a follow-up shot to make sure.

Bolan took off down the hall the instant the British cop fired her last round, pausing only long enough to turn on his own machine pistol's light and give a cursory sweep of the area he'd entered.

"You got him," Bolan called back.

Something round, hard and metallic bounced into the room. Bolan recognized the sound of a grenade hitting concrete from far too many previous encounters.

He whirled for cover, feeling the hammer blow of the shock wave strike him.

TERN HEARD THE DETONATION, and for a brief moment felt a sense of loss as he realized that the enemy who'd come so close to killing him might have died in the fiery eruption of a single grenade. To have been so close to a kill that would have made him feel like a god, and to have it snatched away gave him a moment's hollow pain.

He shook it off. Cooper was alive. There was no way that the grenade could have been a fragmentation bomb—none were kept in the armories for the purposes of defending the tunnels. Their use would have turned the narrow passages and tiny offices into blenders of flying shrapnel for both invader and defender alike. Instead, they had concussion grenades, meant to blind and deafen.

Cooper would be alive for Tern to feel the man's hot blood slick down over his hands. More than the prostitutes, the concept of eviscerating this man, this warrior, filled him with the energy and drive to continue. He charged toward the sound of the battle, scooping an M-16 off the rack. He slipped a magazine into place.

"Where are they?" he asked as he reached a group of his men.

"They're coming in through the northwest branch. We turned them away with a grenade barrage, but they must have brought down some heavy firepower," was the answer.

Tern mentally reviewed his map of the underground caverns. The northwest branch led through the old cubicle farms for the continuity of government officers. There was a side branch that lead around to the old armory, giving either party the opportunity to cut around and blindside their enemy.

"What kind of heavy firepower?" Tern asked.

"We're thinking a 7.62," the SAS renegade said. "Long,

continuous streams of fire means he's got a belt feed for that thing, too."

Tern poked his head out, and saw the glare of a gun-mounted light. He ducked back down and cringed as the wall above his head was pulverized by a salvo of heavy fire. The EAE crew opened up in response, their suppressed rifles and subguns popping incessantly. Heavy slugs walked down the wall and blew apart the man briefing Tern from shoulder to hip, his chest burst open by the brutal NATO slugs that cut through him.

"Fall back!" Tern ordered.

He ripped off a couple of short blasts with his M-16 and retreated. Once on the other side of the door, he hit the release, dropping the bulkhead down. It crushed the remains of the dead man, but at least it stopped the autofire that now rattled harmlessly on the other side of the impregnable steel shielding them.

"We're cutting around," Tern said. "I want two men here, guarding this door, though. The minute the gunfire stops, open it, but stay ready for a renewed fight. I don't need them blowing plastique and bringing down the tunnels on our heads."

Two men quickly took the instructions, and the others spun to follow Tern as he headed for the old armory.

It would prove interesting to see the reaction of his opponents to the new weapons that De Simmones stored there.

It would prove very interesting.

BOLAN STARTED for the door, then stopped. He was still rattled by the concussion wave off the stun-shock grenade, but it wasn't the first time he'd been present at one of these, point blank. He took cover and waved for Smythe to hold off on the gunning.

Dean was at his side, taking cover behind a desk. "What gives?"

"Head back. There's got to be another way around to that tunnel we came through," Bolan said. "They dropped the blast door on us."

"Why does that mean they're coming around? Couldn't they just be trying to cut us off?"

"These tunnels were filled with redundant passageways, in case someone dropped a nuclear weapon over this chunk of the line and collapsed one or two," Bolan explained. "This way, if there were any blocked passages, the survivors could reach each other and not be cut off from important things like food, weapons or medical supplies."

"The mind of a paranoid," Dean muttered.

"I didn't build these things. I've just been in enough of them," Bolan returned. "Smythe, check your six!"

"Already done!" he replied. "Nobody's here yet."

"Right. You stay here. They're going to wait for us to backtrack and look down some side branches," Bolan said.

"When we stop making noise," Smythe said. He popped another round at the steel bulkhead.

"They'll wait, and then come through, probably with a whole kill crew."

"Flank attack," Smythe answered.

Bolan and Dean fell back to where Smythe was settled in.

"You need to cover our backs on this one. No telling what they'll throw through that door," Bolan informed him.

Smythe nodded. "Good luck."

The tall black man killed the gun light under his weapon's barrel and prepared himself. Bolan and Dean took off back in the direction they had come.

THE OLD ARMORY WAS NOW a glass menagerie of sorts, full of women sitting in clear-walled cells. They sat, their faces vacant, bodies kept pretty by the ministrations of De Simmones's handlers. Between indoctrination and the drugs they were given, they were a well-maintained set of weapons, Tern mused.

They were also his shield. He stopped in the room, running his fingers along one plexiglas wall, fingertips squeaking as the polymers dragged on his skin. The zombielike woman sitting in the cell looked up, her mouth open, drool caked at one corner. Her red hair was wild and frizzy, and her brown eyes were bloodshot. He doubted she even had the reflexes to blink, but she proved him wrong when she closed her eyes a moment later.

It wasn't flicker-quick like most blinks, but it was a reaction.

He wondered what was left of the mind inside her skull. He knew that when he attacked, when he laid into Patricia, she was awakening, and she fought back for all she was worth. Not that it had saved her, but it proved that she still possessed a spirit inside the fleshy coffin that De Simmones had made her body into.

"Sir?"

Tern glanced at the man.

"Should we just leave this as scorched earth for the intruders?"

Tern leaned away from the glass. "No. Let the girls live for now. We'll be fine until I deal with Cooper and his companions."

"It was just an idea," the subordinate said.

"Go cut off Cooper. If you can take him alive, do it. If you can't… too bad."

Tern looked into the vacant gaze of the captive girl.

There was always other prey.

ETIENNE DE SIMMONES cursed Liam Tern with every breath. In his fists, he had the black frame of a Heckler & Koch MP-5, its slender barrel supplanted by the piglike snout of a black sound suppressor.

He stopped as he came across a trio of men heading toward the cubicle farm.

"What's going on?" he demanded.

"The intruders are down by the old office complex. Tern closed them in with the bulkhead door, but he wants a team to push through once they've broken off in there."

De Simmones shook his head. "He's going to try to flank them through the old armory?"

The trooper nodded. "We've got six men, if you come with us."

The old vet nodded. "All right. Come on, lads. We'll show this bastard what for."

De Simmones and his men reached the bulkhead and took cover on either side of the doorway. Dousing the lights on their submachine guns, they were plunged into an eerie, murky blackness that unsettled the older vet for a moment. He blinked, trying to get used to the complete lack of vision, then winced as the bulkhead door clanked and creaked. The harsh spill of green fluorescent chemical light crept around the doorway as it opened.

De Simmones crouched deeply, and that was what saved his life. A splash of automatic fire ripped across the doorway at shoulder height, and would have decapitated him. Instead, the defender to his left jerked as his collarbone was nailed with a half dozen slugs. He tumbled facedown to the ground, his machine pistol dropping near De Simmones.

He grabbed up the second weapon and surged forward. De Simmones stayed low to the floor, under the firestorm of hurtling lead. The men behind him fired back, but within seconds, they were dead too, victims of a scythe of heavy-caliber NATO steel that shocked flesh and shattered bone. The machine gun stopped hammering the air.

De Simmones listened to the sound of a bolt opening and rose in one fluid moment. Both guns in his hands opened up, bullets coming out like an extended series of polite coughs from the efficient suppressors. Sparks lit the room, and while the two-gun approach wasted ammunition, it forced the machine gunner to drop his weapon, falling back around the corner with a hissed curse.

The veteran SAS man didn't continue with his charge. He wasn't suicidal and he knew enough that the enemy, while hurt, could have backup weapons to fall back on. He edged closer to the hallway. A quick burst of silenced gunfire informed him that ducking back behind cover was the smart thing to do.

De Simmones reached for a grenade on his harness, armed it then lobbed the bomb around the corner. He yelled to equalize the pressure inside and outside of his head. The detonation went off, shaking him, but not deafening him thanks to his tactic.

He swung around the corner and came face-to-face with Lewis Smythe, holding a big silver handgun. His face was racked with pain, one side darkened with blood. He was still yelling, aiming the muzzle of the Wildey at the center of De Simmones's skull.

With lightning reflexes, De Simmones swung the frame of his machine pistol against the stainless-steel Magnum pistol. At the same time he was able to bring up his other weapon and trigger a point-blank blast into Smythe's belly, hurling him back against the wall.

The big black man staggered, lashed out and fired a shot that fell short of hitting De Simmones, who kicked Smythe in the gut and fired again with his other machine pistol. This time, the tall intruder dropped to his knees, folding over his ravaged guts.

A quick swing of the butt of the machine pistols brought them down on the back of Smythe's head, putting him away.

De Simmones reloaded on the run.

If he was lucky, he might even have a chance to trim Tern from the list of troubles in his life.

17

The Executioner was preceded by the sound of elastic springing, the clatter of cardboard tubing bouncing along concrete. The eruption of light and sound left the gunmen covering their eyes and ears, twisting away from the violent assault on their senses. The shock wave had barely died down when Bolan raced into view, Wildey in one fist, Glock in the other, the gun light under the Glock's barrel spraying the scene of carnage and disarray with a harsh blue-white slash of illumination.

The first target caught in the glare of the spotlight busily fumbled with his machine pistol, but received only a single .44 Automag slug through his head.

Bullets slammed into the wall behind Bolan, and he whipped the Glock around. He didn't bother aligning the sights, the center of the flashlight was filled with the form of the stunned EAE man that fired on him. The gunner still tracked him, but Bolan triggered the Glock 19, sending 9 mm Parabellum rounds chopping through his chest and throat, tearing the fight from him.

A third fighter swung to his feet, but jerked from multiple impacts, his body thrown to the ground as Melissa Dean joined in on the battle. Her machine pistol tore through the man's torso and dropped him onto his back as swiftly as he lunged into view.

The Executioner skidded to a halt and dropped to one knee, avoiding the swung buttstock of a rifle. With a savage punch, he rammed the muzzle of the three-pound Wildey between the man's legs, causing him to scream in agony. He fell over, and Bolan rose as he fell. As the two passed, Bolan punched the man hard across the jaw and heard it crack on impact.

Dean caught up with him.

"That was quick and bloody," she muttered.

"We've got more ahead—" Bolan began to speak.

The sound of explosions and gunfire sounded behind them.

Dean searched Bolan's face for a moment.

"That doesn't sound good. Smythe may be hurt," she said.

"Head back and help him out," Bolan told her. "But be careful. There might be guards in the tunnels."

"And you?"

"I'm meeting the remaining defenders head-on."

"You're going to clean out the rest of this nest by yourself?"

Bolan shrugged. "I'll catch you later."

The loneliness in his voice stung deep into Dean's chest.

He stalked off into the shadows.

LIAM TERN HEARD THE SOUND of the .44 Automag being touched off, instants after a grenade detonation. A few moments later, as if in an echo, another one-two blast occurred grenade and heavy magnum.

He reached into his double shoulder holsters and withdrew the Berettas. He was standing behind a Plexiglas cell. Through the clear armored glass, he saw the form of the his adversary enter into the old armory, leading the way with the Glock.

"Hello again," Tern welcomed him.

"Tern."

Bolan sidestepped, but the Ripper kept the Plexiglas cell between him and the Executioner. The two fighters orbited the cube, the woman inside standing ramrod still, her face slack with drugged stupor.

"You won't shoot through her to get to me. And your weapons don't have the punch to get through this before I can start killing these worthless bags."

"How do you know I won't?" Bolan asked.

"Because you didn't even bother to warn me before you shot me in the back. You saw me murder a woman, and you shot me in the back like a coward. You think these meatbags are actually worth saving."

"I was removing trash. I should have put a bullet into your face."

Tern chuckled. "And then what? All this wonderful warfare would have gone to waste."

Tern cocked the hammers on his Berettas. He leveled one at a glass wall of a cell and fired. The armor-piercing bullet went through the glass and through the arm of a drugged woman. She jerked with a spasm of feeling, then blood poured down from the wound. "KTW armor-piercing rounds. Tungsten core. They'll go through body armor, and they'll go through the prisons these brainless bitches are in," Tern said, laughing.

"But you don't want them," Bolan said.

"Who do I want?" Tern asked.

"Me. You want to finally kill someone to call your own. You're dressed like Jack the Ripper, but you want someone in your own image. Your own personal kill."

Tern smirked. "Drop your guns."

"You think I'm insane?" Bolan asked.

Tern laughed. "You're as loony as I am. After all, who's the one who came down into these tunnels without an entire special operations platoon?"

"How do you know I don't have them looking in other tunnels?" Bolan asked.

"Because you've been taking De Simmones's operation apart all alone. They didn't come across on the train with you, and you moved too quickly to be anything but a small force. Three people, five tops."

Bolan glared.

"Put the guns down. I want to see a knife in your hand, or my next shot goes through a head."

The Executioner let his guns drop to the floor. The grin of the Ripper grew with each clatter of metal on stone.

DEAN SAW DE SIMMONES at the same time he saw her, and they both dived for cover. Bullets sprayed from their weapons, raking the walls, impacts against stone ringing loudly as concrete pulverized under hyper-velocity strikes.

Dean flinched from the assault of stony splinters peppering her face. She tucked in tighter against the buttress that protected her. Bullets hammered at the outcropping, kept her trapped. She sensed that the angle of the impacts had changed. Her opponent was advancing on her, and she was stuck, kept under a constant stream of accurate fire that could tear her arm off if she exposed it.

With a half-turn, she plucked a flash-bang grenade from her harness. She knew that being on top of the bomb would make it agonizing, but it was better to be half deaf and blind than full of lead.

The autofire continued as De Simmones drew closer.

"What's wrong, girlie? Afraid to come out and face the lead?"

The pin came out of the safety lever on the grenade. It sounded like De Simmones was only an arm's length away. One quick lunge, and it would all be over. She had to act fast. She popped the spoon and threw it down at her feet.

"What the hell—"

Dean had only felt these bombs go off when she had the

luxury of tens of feet between her and their detonations. At close range, it was as if a nuclear explosion went off, her eyes and ears melting into one fused mass of agonized slag. She stumbled out from behind her outcropping, flailed for contact, and grabbed hold of De Simmones's harness.

There was a muffled growl and curse, and a fist smashed into the side of her head. Senses numbed by the blast, she didn't feel the impact so much, which was a small favor, but she had to get into the fight fast. She reached out and clawed at the enemy's face.

He returned the favor by poking her in the gut and pulling the trigger. Hot and heavy impacts rumbled all along the wall of Kevlar over her abdomen, and she felt pain. It felt as if boiling water had poured down her stomach and her legs gave out under her. As she went down, she felt the frame of the machine pistol between her breasts. If he managed to angle the gun over her heart, no amount of armor would protect her. She snaked her arm around the gun and twisted her body. The weapon popped free from his grasp and she scrambled backward.

De Simmones's foot came out of nowhere and snapped across her chin, making her head spin. With a surge of energy, she got to her feet. Her vision cleared enough to spot the other machine pistol the SAS vet held. He brought it up, but Dean chopped at his forearm. The gun dropped from his fingers as the two of them crashed against the wall.

She powered an elbow against his face and felt the lump of his cheekbone grate against her joint. With a desperate burst of energy, she attacked the older man's knee with a kick to take him off balance. Her abdomen still felt like hammered potatoes, and she wondered what kind of injuries she had.

De Simmones pushed her away, and she toppled to the floor. Wincing in pain, she saw the man reach for his Walther. Her hand dropped immediately to the Wildey on her thigh.

He pulled his gun free at the same instant she ripped her weapon out of its holster.

The Walther's .32-caliber bullet caught her in the shoulder, stinging far less than anything else she'd felt so far.

The recoil of the Wildey shocked her, but not as much as it shocked De Simmones. He slammed into the wall, his chest caved in by the high-powered bullet.

De Simmones slid down the wall, his eyes staring glassily at her.

"That's for my sister, cocksucker," she said before she slumped against the wall.

LEWIS SMYTHE HURT, the coughs that accompanied his halting attempts at breathing spiked knives of agony through his guts. The Kevlar armor he wore had protected him from being killed, but he needed to get to a doctor.

It wouldn't be as bad as some of the other times. The time when the drug dealers pressed hot knives flat against his skin. They only touched his face once, and left him both his eyes so that he could forever look on the scar of wreckage they left behind.

There was no way he was going to die on a cold concrete floor in the middle of the Maginot Line.

He staggered to his feet and saw the form of a slender young woman enter his vision. He didn't think there were any women on De Simmones's staff, but he reached for his Glock. He was relieved to hear the voice of Melissa Dean.

"Smythe?"

"I'm alive," he answered. He didn't sound as good as he felt, and he felt like hell.

"I saw De Simmones. I killed him."

"You put your ghost to rest then?" Smythe asked her.

"Enough to worry about other priorities. Come on, we have to find Cooper."

She slipped her shoulder under his arm and helped him up. Smythe was glad for someone to lean on.

BOLAN LET THE LAST GUN clatter to the floor.

"One thing," he said. "I just need to know who ordered the killing of Carrington."

Tern tilted his head. "Why?"

"When I win, I intend to bring him to justice."

"You're doing this all for altruism?"

"Duty to my fellow man. I'm a soldier. My job is to protect my country, and ultimately all my country's allies."

Tern cackled. "Don't be a buffoon. We protected your country's secrets with our operations."

"Secrets that need the blood of innocents aren't worth keeping."

Tern palmed his pistols. "Regardless. De Simmones took out Carrington because he actually put two and two together, putting out a time line linking my glorious Ripper killings with the deaths of those who could expose our country's deepest secrets."

"Glorious killings. That's a sick term, but then, look who you're dressed as."

Tern gestured with the muzzle of his pistol up and down at Bolan in his own blacksuit. "You're a fine one to talk."

"De Simmones has the name of his contact in his office. It's the nice pad halfway down the hallway. It's a colonel in British Military Intelligence."

Tern dumped his two sets of Berettas to the ground.

"Fun time, Mr. Cooper."

"I never call this fun," Bolan answered.

The knife dropped from Tern's forearm sheath into his hand with a sudden flick of his wrist. Bolan ripped his combat knife, an Applegate-Fairbairn AF-11, from its spot on his harness.

They stepped clear of the cubicles with the drugged women, and Bolan felt glad for that. He didn't know what condition the cells were in, and didn't want to crash through them with the weight of two grown men, injuring one of the helpless, zombified victims.

Tern feinted forward, but Bolan didn't react to the movement. The Ripper closed the distance a little more, his eyes never leaving the cold blue gaze of the Executioner. The two men were focused on each other, and Bolan knew that a single error would give Tern the edge he needed to eviscerate him.

The Ripper slashed his knife again, slicing high, then bringing his blade down low, catching the Executioner just above the knee. Bolan tugged his leg out of the way in time to prevent a serious cut and speared down with his knife, catching the sleeve of Tern's knife hand, cutting through. Tern pulled back, rubbing his injured arm, then looked at the sheen of blood on the palm of his leather glove.

He brought it to his mouth and licked up the center of his hand, his eyes never leaving Bolan's. "Good vintage."

"I wouldn't know," Bolan replied. He presented himself to Tern edge on, leaving his unscratched leg forward. Blood trickled into the material of his bodysuit, spreading its warmth. He squeezed his knife's handle tighter.

Tern lunged again, and Bolan instantly altered his footing, bringing his left arm up and sweeping aside the knife with a blocking chop. Bolan snaked his leg between Tern's, but the Ripper leaped away from the Executioner's attempt to trip him up. A hard knee stroke caught Bolan on the hip, but Tern received a back fist across the jaw.

They pulled away from each other, but still stayed focused like a pair of savage beasts. Tern danced behind a cell, scraping his knife along the Plexiglas to create an odd squeal.

"Nice moves."

Bolan didn't respond to the comment. Instead, he brought

his knife back in tight to his body, eyes narrowed. He extended his free hand.

Tern lashed his cape out, the rustle of fabric filled the air. Bolan was blinded for a moment as the flash of the cape caught him across the eyes, but he spun out of the way, feeling Tern's blade open a crease in his side even through the Kevlar. The Ripper lashed backward, catching the Executioner across the face again, but Bolan caught a handful of the cloak and tugged hard. Tern's knife sliced again and caught him on the forearm, driving him back.

"Useful. Kept you from blowing me to hell with your pistol, and gave me two free cuts on you. No wonder fencers used to wear capes," Tern said.

"Fancy that," Bolan answered dryly.

Tern attacked again, his cape snapped like a whip, but this time, Bolan stayed out of its range and avoided the point of the Ripper's knife. The Executioner backed against a cell. The Ripper gave a cackle and slashed forward, but Bolan ducked. The cloak snagged on the open top of the cube he'd backed against. Bolan speared forward, shoulder ramming Tern in the chest while he blocked the knife. The Executioner drove the Ripper backward, cape tearing away from his grip and from around his neck.

The two of them toppled to the ground in a jumbled heap, Bolan's knife scratching an ugly furrow across Tern's forehead. Blood spilled into Tern's eye and he twisted away from the blade, but Bolan wrenched hard, clipping the Ripper's chin with his fist. Tern surged, throwing Bolan's weight off of him, and both men rolled away from each other.

Tern got to his feet first, but Bolan pivoted on his back, legs lashing against the Ripper's, knocking him to the ground. Tern was vulnerable to a follow-up ax kick that snapped hard into his rib cage. He coughed, tasting blood from the impact. The Executioner tucked himself tightly and sprung to his feet.

The Ripper looked up from his position on the ground just as Bolan lit into him, and sliced down hard on his chest with his elbow. It didn't have the same power as the Executioner's ax kick, but it still made Tern cough up blood.

A hard punch struck under Bolan's jaw and snapped it aside. With another lash, Tern sliced, the blade deflecting off the Executioner's shoulder. The Ripper drew blood again, but the Kevlar of Bolan's body armor kept it to a mere scratch.

Bolan head-butted Tern, breaking his nose and causing blood to squirt into his eyes. A follow-up punch struck the Ripper under his armpit. With a yank, he pulled the serial killer over and kicked him into a cubicle.

Tern gave a screech as his spine cracked against the corner of the cell, unyielding Plexiglas bending him painfully backward. Bolan surged forward and kicked him in the groin, then followed up with a kick to the chest.

Another hard kick smashed across the Ripper's lips and jaw, ripping flesh and forcing shards of teeth through the shredded skin. Tern reached out and snagged Bolan's ankle, but the Executioner dropped onto his butt, kicking Tern in the jaw again.

This blow stilled Tern. He slumped on the floor, a puddle of blood forming beneath his ruined nose and mouth.

Bolan rose unsteadily to his feet.

He staggered over to the cell and looked in at the woman whose arm Tern had shot. She was bleeding a lot, and he grabbed up the Wildey. He shot off the lock and the clear door swung open.

Bolan fumbled on his harness for his first-aid kit, getting out a stack of bandages and gauze pads. He applied the gauze over the entry and exit wounds, then wrapped the woman's arm in the bandage, applying pressure on the two bullet holes. Blood soaked through the gauze, but stopped as the bandage held in place. It wouldn't last long, and he needed something for the cuts he'd received.

He wondered idly if Dean was all right.

He heard the rustle of fabric behind him, and spun.

Tern's weight fell across Bolan's forearm, leaning hard against him.

"You're not done with me yet," the Ripper said, slurring.

Bolan whirled and chopped him across the jaw with his elbow. With a grab, he went for the Wildey, but Tern stopped him. The two men wrestled frantically for control of the handgun. Bolan stomped Tern's instep, crushing his foot bones.

Tern curled in pain, then jerked his skull against Bolan's jaw. The two men slipped apart again. Bolan raised the Automag, but Tern slammed the door on Bolan's wrist. The impact didn't knock the gun from his grasp, but it did throw his aim off. One cell's wall shattered in a thousand cubes of broken glass. The woman on the other side stepped back, but was unharmed.

Bolan snaked himself deeper into the cell, protecting the woman inside with his own body as he saw the Ripper reach for his armor-piercing Beretta.

Bolan swung the Wildey again and fired twice, destroying the door with the first shot. The second round struck Tern in the chest. He staggered to the floor, but continued to aim his Beretta at the Executioner.

"I'm taking you to hell with me, you bastard!" Tern challenged.

The Executioner adjusted his aim and tripped the Wildey's trigger a third time.

The jacketed hollowpoint round screamed out of the five-inch barrel, striking Tern at eyebrow level, peeling his skull open. Bone shattered and brains splattered on the glass cell behind him, and the Ripper slumped lifelessly to the ground.

Bolan moved over to the motionless corpse. He kneeled and tested the man's throat and found no pulse.

Liam Tern, the modern-day Ripper, was dead.

Epilogue

The colonel took a sip of his brandy and looked around the club. The music was provided by a pianist accompanied by a sultry lounge singer who slinked atop the piano as if she were making love to it. He smirked, enjoying the sight of her pure sexuality on display, the view of her breasts straining against the fabric. The colonel temporarily entertained the thought of getting her to come with him to a room he'd rented for the night, but figured she'd be too high profile. Too many people would keep their eyes on her, and perhaps recognize him as he cheated on his wife.

The colonel cursed his luck and sat back when a woman sidled up to him at the bar. He studied her features. They were strong, not soft and delicate. The first word that came to his mind was handsome. Her hair was clipped short, almost boyish, and he wondered why she went for such a severe look. She wore a turtleneck that hugged her body, and she sat down, crossing her legs under a herringbone tweed skirt, nylon stockinged legs peeking out seductively from calf-length black leather boots.

The colonel smiled.

His luck was improving.

"Hello, love."

She looked him over with cold blue eyes. "Hello to you too. Don't I know you?"

The colonel shook his head and slid her a fifty-pound note. "No."

She palmed the money and smiled dazzlingly. "Sorry. Call me crazy."

"All right, Crazy."

"What can I call you?"

"Call me Sugar Daddy."

"Yummy."

She took a sip of her drink. "So what are you waiting for tonight?"

"A bird like you. You?"

"Waiting for a shot at a big spender looking for love." She batted her eyes. He felt his loins tighten.

"I have a room upstairs."

She looked down at his hand, at the ring on his finger. "The wife's not going to miss you?"

"She thinks I'm out of town with some old mates of mine for a weekend. We have days before she'd be worried."

The colonel laid down another fifty-pound note. She took this just as readily. She leaned in closer. "Follow me, then."

"Follow you? But I'm the—"

She scraped her fingernail under his chin, then slid off her stool. The colonel followed her without further commentary. They passed through to the lobby, where a tall man in black was standing in the narrow stairwell. As he brushed past the man in black, cold, icy eyes caught his.

The woman stopped and smiled.

"You had Carrington killed. My sister died investigating why you had him offed," she told him. Dean looked around. Nobody was in the lobby yet, so she had time. "We found out about the deal you made to have Carrington killed before he could finish the series of articles pointing out your deal with the French to create a cleanup crew to cover up your government's little embarrassments. You tried to clean up your problems with cold-blooded murder, killing my sister in the process."

The colonel lunged at Melissa Dean. She swung her leg and knocked his feet out from under him. The man fell in an awkward heap at the bottom of the stairs, his neck clearly broken. Dean crumpled the fifty-pound notes and dropped them on his chest.

With that, she joined Mack Bolan in leaving the crooked master of De Simmones and his Ripper to die alone.

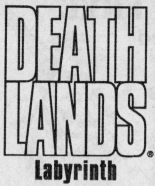

DEATH LANDS®

Labyrinth

In a ruined world, the past and the future
clash with frightening force...

NO TIME TO LOSE

It took only minutes for human history to derail
in a mushroom cloud—now more than a century later, whatever destiny lies ahead for humanity is
bound by the rules that have governed survival since the dawn of time: part luck, part skill and part
hard experience. For Ryan Cawdor and his band, survival in Deathlands means keeping hold of what
you have—or losing it along with your life.

BORN TO DIE

In the ancient canyons of New Mexico, the citizens of Little Pueblo prepare to sacrifice Ryan and his
companions to ancient demons locked inside a twentieth-century dam project. But in a world where
nuke-spawned predators feed upon weak and strong alike, Ryan knows avenging eternal spirits
aren't part of the game. Especially when these freaks spit yellow acid—and their creators are the
whitecoat masterminds of genetic recombination, destroyed by their mutant offspring born of sin and
science gone horribly wrong....

In the Deathlands, some await a better tomorrow, but others hope it never comes....

James Axler
Outlanders®

The war for control of Earth enters a new dimension...

REFUGE

UNANSWERABLE POWER

The war to free postapocalyptic Earth from the grasp of its oppressors slips into uncharted territory as the fully restored race of the former ruling barons are reborn to fearsome power. Facing a virulent phase of a dangerous conflict and galvanized by forces they have yet to fully understand, the Cerberus rebels prepare to battle an unfathomable enemy as the shifting sands of world domination continue to chart their uncertain destiny...

DEADLY SANCTUARY

As their stronghold becomes vulnerable to attack, an exploratory expedition to an alternate Earth puts Kane and his companions in a strange place of charming Victoriana and dark violence. Here the laws of physics have been transmuted and a global alliance against otherwordly invaders has collapsed. Kane, Brigid, Grant and Domi are separated and tossed into the alienated factions of a deceptively deadly world; one from which there may be no return.

Available at your favorite retailer.

GOLD EAGLE

GOUT36

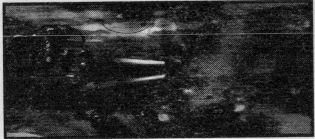